*The Tempered Wind*

# JEANNE DIXON

# *The Tempered Wind*

ATHENEUM
NEW YORK   1987

Atheneum
Macmillan Publishing Company
866 Third Avenue, New York, NY 10022
Collier Macmillan Canada, Inc.

Type set by PennSet, Inc., Bloomsburg, Pennsylvania
Printed and bound by Fairfield Graphics, Fairfield, Pennsylvania
Designed by Suzanne Haldane
First Edition

10  9  8  7  6  5  4  3  2  1

Library of Congress Cataloging-in-Publication Data
Dixon, Jeanne.
    The Tempered wind.

    Summary: Orphaned and unwanted Gabriella, suffering from
all the painful physical and emotional ramifications of dwarfism,
accepts a job as a chore girl with a family in Montana where she
finds love, disappointment, and, most importantly, independence.
    [1. Dwarfs—Fiction.  2. Orphans—Fiction.  3. Montana—
Fiction]  I. Title.
PZ7.D6444Te  1987      [Fic]      87-1379
ISBN 0-689-31339-X

*For my friend Linda,*
*through sunlight and shadow.*

# The Tempered Wind

# 1

Throughout all of my seventeen years on this earth, I had never seen any two people in love. Not really in love. Not like in novels, that kind of love. My parents had always been strict about things, like having good posture, like chewing each bite twenty times before swallowing, but if they had ever been in love with each other, they never let on.

My parents were good people, both of them. I can say that now without the old bitterness that used to consume me. They cared for each other sensibly and without any great show, just as they always cared for me. My father worked first at a furniture store, later a bank. My mother, a quiet dark-haired woman, kept the house tidy and forever drew the curtains so the carpet wouldn't fade. She had supper

3

on the table every evening at six, read aloud from the Scriptures every evening at seven.

I can never imagine them chasing each other through fields of red poppies—two bright butterflies let out at noon—the way Tasha and her Nils Halvorson would do. It was from Tasha and Nils, not my dear parents, that I gained my first understanding of all that is meant by falling in love: the tenderness, passion, and pain.

When I was twelve my father died suddenly of a stroke—and not at home in my mother's bed. All of this was very hush-hush, and for a whole year afterward my mother wore black, though she did not mourn. My life, if you could call it life, went on as always, with one day following another in humdrum procession. You see, for my own protection, I was not allowed to step one foot out the door. Not ever. Not since the day of my birth, not even once would they let me go out—not after they discovered just what kind of creature I was, and what I would never become.

My parents fed me, dressed me, and kept me clean.

As soon as I was able, I tried to bathe myself. I stood in front of the upstairs sink, while my mother held the chair so it wouldn't tip and spill me to the floor. I was not allowed to bathe in the big white tub with the lion's-claw feet, for fear I'd fall and bump my head and drown. And then they wouldn't have me anymore, they said. And who would be to blame?

While my father was alive he took some pleasure in teaching me simple computation—"to give her something to do"—he told my mother. And he was the one who hoisted me onto his shoulders and trotted me down the stairs for the evening meal and my mother's Scripture readings.

4

The stairwell was steep and narrow, I remember, and in memory it seems to have been as dark and disheartening as a sleepless night, and filled with the twitterings of bats. This last I know could not have been true, for my parents abhorred anything that appeared to be threatening, or strange. They would have exterminated bats.

After Father passed on, Mother brought all my meals to my room and read Scripture aloud while I ate my boiled beef with bread. With this change in my schedule my world shrank, diminishing to the size of my bedroom, which was just large enough for my single cot, a chest of drawers, a desk and lamp, and a bookcase full of books.

The books had been willed to my father by some long-departed uncle, and it was obvious that no one had ever read them because many of the pages had not been cut through. To get at what was written in them, I had to tear through the pages myself. Had it not been for these books, I shudder to think what my life might have been—less than human, surely.

William Cullen Bryant, Wordsworth, Whittier, Coleridge . . . oh, so many books of poetry. And novels by Mark Twain, Charles Dickens, Corelli— *Wormwood*—and a copy of *Black Beauty*—that wonderful book about horses—and another every bit as wonderful, called *Beautiful Joe* . . . and I must not forget *Rosa's Quest* . . . and one of my very favorite stories, *My Brown-Eyed Young Man,* by Maria Easterland Gluck. How I loved them!

When I was five my mother taught me to read, and reading became my only source of knowledge about the world outside my room. I longed to befriend a poor mangled cur like Beautiful Joe. I longed to gallop a horse like Black Beauty. I longed to flirt behind a fan, to ride a raft down the Mississippi, to

5

love and to be loved like Rowena LeSage in *My Brown-Eyed Young Man*. Apart from these characters, I would have had no life at all, so my mind clung to details of *life* as these stories portrayed it. My imagination grew by leaps and bounds. *I* did not.

"Unlike less fortunate children," my mother pointed out, I did have a room of my own, for which I ought to be grateful. And I had a door that locked . . . locked from the outside only, of course. Locked for my own protection, of course. Of course.

Above my desk a small, spidered window offered a spidered view of the sky. Mother explained that that was where God the Father had his home, on the other side of the window bars, up there in the sky, in the company of his saints and angels. She said that that was where Father had taken up residence, too. On this point of theology she sounded somewhat doubtful. "We must pray for him," she said grimly. "Every day of our lives we must pray for your father's immortal soul."

I promised I would, but did not.

On the afternoon of my thirteenth birthday, my mother was struck and killed by a bus as she crossed a busy intersection near our home in St. Louis, and I was given to the care of an old Aunt Charlotte, a stupid woman with watery eyes, who gave me to another aunt, who really didn't want me. She passed me on to Tante Eloise, who didn't want me, either.

Not that I blamed her. I never had been a beautiful child. But then neither, I think, had she. *Tante* Eloise, as she asked to be called, gently informed me that the word *tante* was simply a different and lovelier way of saying *aunt*. She was a tall, thin woman with sallow skin and yellowed hair. Her face hung in folds, yet her yellowed curls stayed perfectly in place, as if they'd been set there with glue when Tante was in her teens. I did not expect to like this aunt much, but at that time in my life I did not much like anyone.

"Poor little thing," said Tante Eloise, looking down at me. "Poor dear little thing."

I'd been plunked down in a wingback chair in the darkened parlor, waiting for the driver to carry in my suitcase and my box of life-sustaining books. I clenched my jaws and stared at the carpet, all too well aware that my slippered feet did not touch the floor. There was nothing I could do to hide this fact.

Tante Eloise wore rimless spectacles covered with a fine film of dust. "What am I going to do with you, Gabriella? I'm too old to have to raise a child." She spoke without malice, and she smiled on me kindly to set me at ease.

"I'm thirteen," I said, "almost an adult. You won't have me on your hands very long. I can do simple computations and I've read a good deal. For my age I am very responsible, and I'll soon be on my own."

"My dear little girl, you don't really expect to be on your own."

"I'm nearly grown up, it won't be long."

"Grown up?" Her face went from concerned benevolence to amazed disbelief. "You don't really expect that you will ever grow up."

"There are lots of ways of growing up," I said, repeating the stableman's observation in *Black Beauty*. "It doesn't mean just growing tall."

Tante Eloise drew a hanky from the sleeve of her black crepe dress. She dabbed first at her eyes, then her nose. "What courage," she said when she was able to speak. "How brave you must be. But tell me, what will you do when you're all grown up? What kind of work will you be suited for, dearest child? What kind of life do you expect to lead?"

"The best," I said, thinking of Rowena LeSage. "The very best."

She shoved the hanky back up her sleeve and gave me a short, quick smile. "The good Lord knew what he was doing when he sent you to me. I've needed someone to think about besides myself. I have been too self-centered of late. Much too much wrapped up in grief. There is nothing," she murmured, "half so selfish as sorrow." Her eyes filled again. "You are such an inspiration, *chérie*. When I see how cheerfully you bear your cross . . ." Here she stopped and stared at the tips of my olive drab slippers, which were still a long way from touching the floor. "When I see how well you bear your cross, it gives me the strength to bear mine."

*Glad to be of service*, I thought—but held my tongue. It's always my mouth that gets me in trouble.

The driver who had carried me in from the taxi (because it was raining, and because I had no shoes) reappeared in the doorway, my suitcase tucked under his arm. " 'Escuse me, mum, but where do you want I should put this?"

Tante Eloise waved him toward the basement door. "Down there. But not on the bed. Mind the light and the stairs."

"Now, where was I?" She wore the merest hint of frown.

"Cross-bearing."

"Oh, yes . . . when I lost my Walter I truly believed that my life had come to its end. But now, seeing you . . . so much more to be pitied . . ." She pressed her face with her hanky. When she regarded me again, her old eyes shone with a newness of life, and for a moment I was afraid she might hug me. I'd been hugged to death by old Aunt Charlotte, and I'd learned that people will hug you and hug you

8

when they don't know what else to do with you. I learned well and early not to trust huggers and I still don't trust them.

The cabbie was back in the doorway. "Escuse me, mum, but there's a big box of books. Where do you want I should put them?"

"Put them in Gabriella's room. Where else? Put them in the basement with the suitcase."

"That box is fearful heavy, mum. I don't think I can carry it, not by myself."

"Then carry the books in by the armload, please. Neither my niece nor I is in any shape to help you."

He touched his cap. "Thank you, mum."

*"Il n'y a pas de quoi."*

I watched as he carried them in: Black Beauty prancing along with the pony Merry Legs, Beautiful Joe with his poor cropped ears and docked tail, Tom Sawyer whitewashing his fence, David Copperfield, Little Nell . . . all my friends, all the friends I'd ever known, not to forget my brown-eyed young man and his lady love, Rowena LeSage. Nor the castaways from another wonderful novel, *A Strange Manuscript Found in a Copper Container.* In my aunt's house I might be a castaway, but I'd never be alone.

*"Enchantée,"* murmured Tante Eloise, as she watched them come in. The cabby had carried in the last load of books and had gone back to his cab for the carton. "I can see that you read," Tante said brightly. "That must help you pass the hours. And here . . . here what a lovely big carton, you can use that for a table down there in your room. I hope you don't mind that I can't ask you to share quarters upstairs with me, for there simply isn't any room. And it will be nicer for you in the basement, your own little domicile . . . a *garçonnière,* don't you see?"

She thanked the driver, paid him, then helped

me down the stairs to my new home. She clutched my hand and warned me which step could be trusted, which step was loose. "My Walter always took care of repairs. I don't know what I'll ever do without him."

Unlike my room at my parents' house, the basement room was spacious, though dark. Gray cement walls wept rivulets, with no provocation that I could discern. Against one weeping wall stood a cot illuminated by a single naked light bulb descended from a beam. In addition to these furnishings, there was a cracked washbasin with a cold water tap turning green, that and a brownish commode without a cover.

"Well?" said Tante Eloise. "What do you think?"

"*Enchantée*," I said, not missing a beat. "It is simply *enchantée*."

"I hope it will do. I had such short notice . . ." She looked askance at my suitcase and books, as though they somehow plucked a wrong note in the harmony of her decor. "I'm not a wealthy woman, you know."

"It was kind of you to take me in."

"You're quite welcome, *ma fille*. I see it as my duty as a Christian."

At this my mind grew dark. My hands, heart, thoughts turned instantly to ice. Duty? Was that all I was ever to be?

"Christians must be truly dutiful people," I said.

Pure sarcasm, and I knew it. And I had no excuse except that of viciousness, sheer viciousness. I was tired from my trip, it's true; but more than that I was tired of packing up and moving on from aunt to aunt. I was tired of having to be grateful. Other children ran out into the sunshine to play beneath the trees. Other children had mothers and fathers who loved them, doted on them, fed them, clothed them, kept them from loneliness, woke them with kisses. I had seen other children, had glimpsed them from windows, heard them at play, and I'd read all about them in books. Rosy-cheeked, sparkling-eyed, with their toys and their games and their friendships, they filled me with envy, an envy that threatened to turn into rage. I was not a nice person—and I knew it—but I tried to keep this fact secret. I held back my rage and I smiled, and smiled.

"Poor little thing," my aunt said, as I smiled her way. "You probably know nothing of religion. Have you ever been to church? No . . . I'd think not, not in your condition. And tell me, have you ever been to school?"

"No. Never." All this, still smiling.

"Oh. My dear." Light from the overhead bulb shone down on her stuck-in-place curls. I dropped my gaze to her neatly shod feet parked so primly on the damp cement floor. "Oh, my dear . . ." she went on. "Oh, my dear, dear . . . *dear*."

I wanted to flee, but where?

I hoisted myself up onto the cot—all thirty-seven and one-half inches of me—and listened to her plans.

"First," she said, "we must do something about your hair. It is dreadful, simply awful, that carroty color and straight as a rope. Whatever could your parents have been thinking of? Then we must see to your clothing. Appearance is so all-important, you know. Then, when we are readied, we must start you in at the Young Ladies' Christian Academy. My Walter was a French teacher there, and a better class of people you would never want to meet."

She brought a straight chair down from the kitchen and had me stand on it. "Such a little thing," she said, "so oddly proportioned, yet . . ." As she spoke, she studied me all around—front, sides, back, front again—until I felt like a housefly pressed under a glass. "Never let it be said that your Tante Eloise raised you up to be a heathen. When I was your age I wanted to be a missionary—Borneo, Java, Africa, Spain—but I married my Walter and served him instead. It is something I've always maintained: True Christian charity must begin at home."

I smiled and smiled, and I turned myself around for her closer inspection.

As it was already past suppertime, Tante Eloise excused herself and hurried upstairs to set the kettle boiling. She came back down with a hand-embroidered tablecloth—something my mother had made years ago, as a girl. Tante spread it over the carton that had held my books. The tablecloth design was worked in cross-stitch, a garden scene of the Old South. A young woman, a Southern belle, waited languidly beneath a willow, while her young lover on the far end of the cloth came racing toward her, mounted on a cross-stitch hunter.

I touched the red threads of the peonies in the garden, the blue threads for bluebells, purple for larkspur. The woman's hair was glossy black, her hoopskirts silky and rainbow-hued.

While I examined this work of art, Tante Eloise had gone upstairs and returned with a sandwich and a cup of milky tea on a tray. "I do hope you like chopped egg sandwiches."

"Oh, me," I said. "I do." I smiled to show how very much I liked them.

"I eat the same thing every evening, every evening a chopped egg sandwich. That way I never have to wonder what to cook." To my lack of response, her face assumed a bulldog expression. "If you like I could find you something else. A juicy dill pickle?"

"No, thank you. This is lovely. Thank you." Smile.

"I could run down to the store and buy you something special . . . ?"

"Oh, no."

"Are you sure? I could take the money I have in my purse . . ."

"No. This is exactly perfect." Smile. "Thank you."

"You're sure, now?"

"I'm sure." My face ached from so much smiling, but that didn't stop me. I smiled more and more.

Before she left, she showed me how to pull the light string to turn the overhead bulb on and off. "Lucky for us it has a long string. You have to pull it twice to turn it off, once to turn it on." She demonstrated. "Pull gently, now. If the string breaks you'll be left in the dark. Here, we'll tie it to the end of the bedframe. If you need to get up in the night you shouldn't have to stumble around in the dark, maybe stub your toe in the bargain."

"You are really very thoughtful, Tante Eloise."

"I try."

The moment she was gone I gobbled my sandwich and downed the cold tea in five short swallows, wiped my mouth on the back of my hand.

The overhead bulb lighted the room with a dingy light. Once again I took in my environs: commode, chair, cot, box. That was all. Not the life I had prayed for.

I didn't feel like reading. I slid my suitcase handily under the cot, arranged my books in stacks on top of the carton, turned out the light, and undressed myself in the dark. For the longest time I lay awake, shivering beneath the dampish bedclothes. I reviewed the events of the day, tried to feel grateful that I had a new home. I could have been dumped on the street. I could have been placed in an institution. But no. I was warm and safe with this latest

13

of aunts, I still had my books, and she said that I might go to school.

"God," I prayed, shutting my eyes against the smothering dark, "I don't know what plans you've got for me, but so far none of your plans have worked out. Sometimes I think you must have forgotten me, or else they're wrong when they say that you're a god of love. Sometimes it seems as if you just don't care."

"Have faith," my mother used to say. "One of these days His plans for you will be revealed." She said she had some questions she wanted to ask, too.

"If you and I could change places," I told Him, "I would never have done anything as cruel as you have done to me." He knew what I meant, we'd discussed this problem so many times before. "I am just a mortal, full of doubts and fears. Ignorance, too. But I would never have done this to *you*. Really, God, you ought to be ashamed. Amen."

That night I dreamed about Beautiful Joe. His ears and tail had just been docked by his cruel master. The moment I saw him I fell down beside him, to cradle his poor bloodied head in my arms. He wagged his tail, looked up at me, and fell over dead . . . out of fright at what he saw, I imagine. I was not a pretty sight. Babies sometimes scream when they see me. I woke that first night in a state of terror. "Oh, God!" I cried out against that thick, sour darkness. "I've tried so hard not to complain. I've tried so hard to know your Will. Why have you done this to me? It's not *fair*."

Certain that no one could hear, I sobbed aloud, rocking back and forth in my pain. "All I ask is a place to belong to, someone to love. Is that too much? Is it?"

14

I felt the press of dark against my face. And silence. "Why can't you answer me?"

Silence.

And did He answer me?

Oh, no, not Him.

Not then.

## 2

Out of the frying pan, into the fire:

That was my life at the Young Ladies' Christian Academy. Oh, not at first. At first it seemed as though all my prayers were at last to be answered. Tante Eloise got all dressed up and came down to my room to tell me her plans. She would go down to her church for "guidance and assistance," and when she came back she would have "suitable clothing for me."

True to her promise, she returned late that afternoon with a basket full of secondhand clothes from the charity box. There was a child's coat, "hardly worn," made from a heavy dark wool. "And this vest should fit you nicely."

She pulled a maroon-colored garment out of the basket and held it up to my face as if it did wonders for my hair and eyes. "It *is* a nice color," she said. "I know you don't want to draw attention to yourself, so I've stuck to the darker shades for you."

She went back upstairs and brought down a plain kitchen chair. "Can you climb up by yourself? Here, let me help you."

Beneath the benediction of the sixty-watt bulb, Tante Eloise dug through the basket of clothing, searching for a "nice white blouse. Oh, I know it's in here somewhere, that and a sweet little skirt. I simply couldn't resist the sweet little skirt."

While I struggled out of the garment that my mother had made, my aunt kept up a happy soliloquy, in which she described the former owners of the clothes she had brought me. Anything was better than what I was wearing. My mother had made my undergarments as well as the dress that I wore. She had made the dress out of a single piece of yardage by cutting a hole for my head and sewing up the sides as far as my arms. She had bought the entire bolt of material on sale, so I had worn the same color year after year; an olive drab, it had as much appeal as a plate of cold spinach.

"Ah," said my aunt, "here it is, the nice white blouse." She held it up for my viewing. "This blouse was worn by one of the children of a woman in my guild, and a nicer little girl you would never want to meet . . . darling, sweet-tempered . . . with, oh, my! such big blue eyes . . . and Shirley Temple curls. And could she sing! And could she tap dance! She could tap dance till the cows came home, and you'd never get tired of her, she was that much entertainment."

I gripped the back of the kitchen chair, while Tante Eloise fitted this miracle of garments first onto my right arm, then onto my left, drawing it close to button in the back. I saw myself with the same blue eyes and the Shirley Temple curls, my poor bent body dancing like a feather tossed up in a breeze. How they would love me, those young ladies of the Christian Academy! How I in turn would love them!

There wasn't any looking glass, so I had to wait for my aunt's reaction.

"Well . . ." she said, then paused. "It doesn't quite come together in the back, not enough to button it. But, *c'est rien*, that won't make any matter, for the back will be covered when we've pulled on the vest."

The vest smelled strongly of napthalene, which Tante Eloise said was used to kill the moths. Nevertheless, there was a penny-size moth hole in the front of the vest, smack in the middle. "*C'est rien*," said Tante Eloise. "We can tuck the vest into the waistband of this sweet little skirt." She smiled on me, her eyes still shining. "If you don't tell, no one will ever be the wiser."

The vest fit snug across the shoulders, and the bottom fell to just above my knees.

My aunt's curls shone an unruffled yellow as she bent over the cot to smooth out the wrinkles of the skirt, which was pleated and purple. Still smiling, she dropped the skirt over my arms, head, and shoulders. It stuck. "Oh," she said. "*Attendez*, we forgot to unzip it."

I waited lily-still while she struggled with the zipper, then pulled the skirt down to what should have been my waistline, if I'd had a waist. It was there that our plans began to sour, for when I saw my aunt's furrowed expression, her glow of endeavor had dimmed. Doubts fluttered through the room like fat gray moths.

The skirt zipped only partway up and wouldn't begin to button.

"We can set the button over," declared Tante Eloise.

The skirt was too long. The pleated purple wool fell almost to my feet.

Tante Eloise's face grew grim. "We can take the scissors, set a new hem."

Fleeting were the big blue eyes, the Shirley Temple curls, the applause . . . the love. "Tante Eloise?"

My aunt had stepped back to take in the effect. "Mmmmm?" she replied, looking hard at the skirt, not at me. "What is it, child? Speak up."

"Tante Eloise, will they . . . you know . . . the young ladies . . . ?" I couldn't get the words out, my throat, my heart were so choked with feeling.

"Will they *what?*" Her penciled eyebrows arched above her eyes. The collar of her dress held flecks of mildew, and I smelled the stale powder in the creases of her neck.

"Will they like me?" I wanted to ask about love, but I settled for like.

"Like you?" she said, showing her small, perfect teeth. "Gabriella, dearest child, of course they will like you. They will *love* you. That's the whole purpose of the academy, to teach true Christian charity for those less fortunate. They will have no choice but to love you."

That wasn't at all what I'd wanted to hear. My voice grew tense and high. "Are you sure? Are you sure they will like me? What if they laugh at me? My shoes . . ." my voice quavered. "I have no proper shoes. I can't go to school, not without shoes." I was wearing the olive drab slippers that my mother had crocheted for me, her last gift before she died. They were cozy and warm, but hardly fit for school.

"Well," said Tante Eloise, "you can't expect to have everything at once, now can you?" She pressed her lips tightly together, cocking her head to one side. Her eyes were the color of bees. "If you hope to get along in this world, Gabriella, you must learn the fine practice of patience." She stopped to let this wisdom sink in. "And a little show of gratitude would not go amiss."

Standing on my chair in that cold, dank basement, the hanging bulb my only hope of sun, my blouse gapping in the back, my vest trailing to my knees, my skirt hiked up to hide the moth hole, I felt like the meanest creature ever imagined. So, I apologized.

"Apologies accepted. Now, if your highness would care to try the coat . . . ?"

The coat was longer than the skirt, and so heavy it could have been a suit of armor, if it had come with a helmet and shield.

"Oh, my dear . . ." Tante Eloise surveyed the effect. "Oh, my dear, dear, dear, dear . . . *dear.*"

It was that bad.

At that time in my life I didn't dare show my true emotions. "Laugh and the world laughs with you," my father had always said. "Weep and you weep alone."

Even so, I know I shed a tear or two when I saw myself in my aunt's eyes, an ugly duckling, trying to dress like a swan in other people's discarded splendor.

Tante Eloise did not like my tears. After all, as she told me, she had tears of her own to shed, and just as much reason to shed them. "As to your appearance, we will do everything we can to make you acceptable. Any more than that should not be expected. *Après tout,*" she said, and her eyes once more began to shine, "it doesn't matter how we look on the outside, it's how we look to the Lord that makes the difference." She smoothed her yellowed curls.

"I just want them to like me." I tried to keep the pain from my voice and failed. "I've never had friends."

"Never mind, never mind . . ." She pressed her lips tightly and frowned as she studied my hair. "What do you think we should do to your head? Pincurls, I'd say, wouldn't you?"

Though the Lord might have been content to overlook my appearance, Miss Rasmussen, headmistress of the Young Ladies' Christian Academy, was not.

White-haired and smiling, she sat behind a cheerfully cluttered desk in a room resplendent with windows, and potted green plants on every sill, soaking up sunshine. Things went well, at first. Miss Rasmussen explained to my aunt that the school would be simply delighted to have any relations of hers enrolled at the academy, "if only for remembrance of our dear departed Walter." My expired Uncle Walter had taught French there, and had been very much admired.

Miss Rasmussen gave me a warm, warm smile. "Such a darling child."

I could see my reflection in the lenses of her glasses, and I couldn't see anything the least bit darling about me. Tante Eloise had done my hair in pincurls, as she'd promised, but the effect was hardly Shirley Temple; and all of us there in Miss Rasmussen's office knew it.

"What a very brave child Gabriella must be," said Miss Rasmussen, after a longer second look. "And how very brave of you, Eloise, to take her on."

Tante Eloise made a sound in her throat and crossed her ankles. She had worn a black dress, a black patent leather belt around her narrow waist, with black patent leather shoes, a black cloth coat with black buttons. A slight touch of rouge blushed her cheeks, and her hair had been coaxed into a marcel wave surrounded by a halo of curls. She gave a tearful little smile. "I want only the best for Gabriella."

"I am sure you do," said Miss Rasmussen, beaming, and the sun shone down upon her shoulders. "However, I must warn you, Eloise, that we have recently instituted a school dress code, so there will be the extra expense of a school uniform."

Tante frowned. "Oh?"

"Should Gabriella attend classes here at the academy, she will have to have a regulation blue jumper, white blouse, plaid tie, white knee socks . . ." She cast a glance at my feet in their olive drab slippers. ". . . and shoes. Regulation black oxfords."

Tante Eloise shrank into her chair.

"You do understand."

"Of course, of course." She sniffed loudly and withdrew her hanky. "But perhaps you can understand my position. I don't mean to complain, but she was left on my doorstep, so to speak, an orphan, uneducated, completely lacking in social graces, nothing in the way of possessions, and I . . . well, as you realize, I have no vast stores of wealth. My Walter left insurance, and I have tried to be frugal, but . . ."

"Believe me, Eloise, we do so sympathize. Naturally, we will waive tuition fees."

"Oh, that would be so very kind."

"Still, there is the matter of a uniform."

Both women stared at me.

"Would it be possible . . ." ventured Tante Eloise, "since Gabriella is such a special person, do you suppose that Miss Havers in home ec might sew up a uniform? Say, as an extra credit project for her girls?"

"Oh," said Miss Rasmussen, and it was her turn to frown. "I don't know if Miss Havers will go along with that. I don't know that she'd go along with that at all."

"But think of it," said my aunt, "think of the lesson the girls would learn from such a project. What an opportunity for an act of loving charity. Oh, it would do the girls good!"

At this point I lost the thread of the argument, not from lack of interest, but because I had heard a bell ring in the building and a moment later there came the soft clatter of footsteps passing in the hallway outside Miss Rasmussen's office. I heard the voices of girls calling to one another, teasing, laughing. Then out on the emerald lawns that stretched for acres and acres in the mid-September sunlight, I saw groups of girls in their regulation blue jumpers, blazers, white socks, black shoes. They appeared to be just my age, laughing, talking, walking arm in arm, knowing each other by name. At that very moment, watching through Miss Rasmussen's office windows, I believed that I could be one of them. I really believed that I could.

"Gabriella?" Miss Rasmussen drew me back gently. "How do you feel about attending the academy?"

"Oh," I cried. "I want to go to school here. More than anything else in the world. I've never wanted anything as much as I want to attend this school."

Miss Rasmussen must have been taken somewhat aback at my enthusiastic reply, but she only smiled. "And how would you feel about Miss Havers's home ec girls taking your measure to sew up a regulation uniform? Would that embarrass you?"

"Oh, no," I said. "I never get embarrassed. Not at all." I gave her my most sincere smile.

"How wonderful of you," said Miss Rasmussen. "It isn't everyone who knows how to accept a handicap, especially anyone as young as you. Though one thing you really must know, Gabriella, is that everyone is handicapped in some way. Sometimes, as in your case, the handicap is external and visible, but often times, the handicap is psychological and invisible, but it is a handicap just the same." She got to her feet, and the sun from the windows shone around her, like glory.

Tante Eloise got to her feet.

I struggled to get out of the chair.

"Is it agreed then?" asked Tante Eloise.

"I shall call Miss Havers," said Miss Rasmussen. "I'm sure that she is in her room. She has this period free. And if she says yes, then you may consider Gabriella enrolled."

My aunt and I waited outside, while Miss Rasmussen talked to the teacher on the office phone, then Miss Rasmussen emerged, looking very happy indeed. We shook hands all around.

When a girl fat as a rain barrel came down to escort me up to the home ec room, where they would take my measurements to make me acceptable clothing, I felt weak. I tried to smile, a real smile, but all I could do was shake.

"This is our Sylvia," the head mistress said. "Miss Sylvia Plus, meet Gabriella Wheeler."

"Hullo," said Sylvia.

"How do you do?" I put out my hand, marking this milestone in the course of my life. I saw Sylvia Plus as my first real friend, human friend, flesh and blood friend. "I'm very glad to meet you," I said.

"Sylvia," said Miss Rasmussen, "shake hands with Gabriella."

With but a slight hesitation, Sylvia did as she was told. "Charmed."

I followed Sylvia slowly, painfully, up the stairs, clutching the banister, hauling myself up each step, waiting, hauling up the next step, yet almost sick with a giddy excitement. Below, I heard Tante Eloise exclaim, "Oh, but are we not fortunate? And think what an opportunity Gabriella will be for the girls!"

"She's a brave little soul," said Miss Rasmussen. "And what an inspiration to us all!"

# 3

It was mid-September of 1946 that I was officially enrolled at the Young Ladies' Christian Academy, a time that I will always remember, if not for the unhappiness that I suffered there, then for the hope that for the very first time burned within me, the hope that I would find a life tailored to my needs; for that was all I thought about then. Everything was me, me, me.

The academy was located at the edge of a fashionable residential district several miles from my aunt's house. It was composed of a lovely grouping of white clapboard buildings situated beneath silvery windtossed trees and surrounded by a high brick wall that one could pass through by means of a black iron gate.

Every morning Tante Eloise left me a shredded wheat biscuit in a cereal bowl, with a cup of milk, outside the door at the top of the basement stairs. There was always a sandwich, too, wrapped in waxed paper. I was not encouraged to use the kitchen, out of fear of what harm I might do there. When I had finished the shredded wheat and milk, I would walk to the bus stop and climb the difficult steel steps into the city bus. I was always self-conscious about looking for a seat, but I always found one. Even on the most crowded mornings, passengers were quick to get up and move back when they saw me look their way. Small children sometimes cried. Sometimes they talked about me, just within my hearing. Their eyes would never meet mine. They said terrible, terrible things.

Up in home ec I had been studied and measured, cooed over by teachers and students alike, and I was soon in possession of a custom-designed jumper, a blouse that fitted me perfectly, a small plaid tie to knot around my neck, and a dark blue blazer with the school's emblem on it. And shoes. When I stuffed newspaper into the shoes to take up the slack, and when I cut the sides with razors to allow for the width—*voilà!* There I was. Acceptable. Me.

Most wonderful of all, the shoes had metal taps, heel and toe, which made the most satisfying sound as I hurried down the sidewalk to the bus stop. It sounds childish, a girl my age, tripping down the sidewalk with taps on her shoes. But I had been kept in isolation so long that every new experience was like a wonderful adventure. I am certain that if my parents had lived I would have spent my whole life in that upstairs room, my every need catered to, except that most urgent need of all—the need to grow up.

Every morning at twenty to nine, I got off the bus at the corner beside the red brick wall of the school. Clouds of pigeons flew up at my approach. Every single morning the same old black woman climbed onto the bus, and the bus ground its gears and roared away. Behind a white-painted bench and drifts of dead leaves, there was a bronze plaque bolted to the academy wall. Hebrews 10:24 ". . . and let us consider one another to provoke unto love . . ."

Directly in front of this plaque Sylvia Plus had taken to waiting, to walk with me through the black iron gate, across the leafy yard, and on to my first class, English, the same as hers.

Sylvia Plus was no more popular than I was. Built like a barrel, she wore her brown hair in a Dutch bob with bangs. Her face was round and puffy, her eyes like narrow slits. If she'd been kind, I could have forgiven her every fault, but she was not. The other girls were quick to notice us as we entered the yard. "Hel-lo, Syl-via," they called in their ringing voices. "Good morn-ing, Gabri-el-la." Then would come the snickering, and Sylvia's face would turn red as mine burned. "There go plus and minus," the girls would cry. And then they'd laugh.

Sylvia ignored them. She walked along, her wash-tub arms curved around her rain-barrel body, as if the other girls weren't there. "Sticks and stones may break my bones," she said, when I asked her if she didn't mind the teasing. "But words can never hurt me."

"You don't have to walk with me if you don't want to." We were on our way from English class to chapel. We could hear the girls whispering and snickering behind us. Each time I turned around they assumed innocent faces, and then they burst into fits of giggling the moment that I turned back. "I can

28

walk to my classes by myself," I told Sylvia. "I don't want you to suffer just because of me."

"It don't matter," she said in her singsong voice. "Nothing really matters if you don't want it to."

"It matters to me."

"Don't let them know it if it does."

Sylvia's face was bland and smooth as a pumpkin, with two dark pumpkin-seed eyes. Her mouth turned up like the letter U. No matter what, she never stopped smiling. I knew her face must ache the way mine did.

As we entered the chapel and found our pew, Sylvia offered me a foil-wrapped chocolate kiss. At first I didn't take it, I didn't know what it was. "Go ahead," she whispered, nudging me with an elbow. "It's not a snake, it won't bite you. Besides, I've got more. Lots more." She showed me a sack of such kisses in the pocket of her blazer. "Just don't tell," she whispered, "and you might get more."

At that moment I slipped the chocolate into my pocket, I glanced up and caught Alice Boshears staring over her shoulder from the pew in front of ours. She gave me a look of sheer malice. Then she nudged the girl sitting next to her, and the two put their heads together, whispering until chaplain got us going in a hymn.

I never do sing; I've been told I have a voice like an asthmatic duck, so I used the singing time to peel back the foil from the chocolate kiss and pop it into my mouth. My goodness, how delicious! My parents had never held with eating sweets, nor had my aunts. Having this succulent volcano-shaped piece of chocolate melting in my mouth was as close to heaven as I had ever been. The remainder of the service was all the sweeter for it, the hymns more buoyant, the prayers more sincere. When at last we filed out for our next-period classes, I went on to European history with more zip and enthusiasm than ever before. I had forgotten Alice and her friend.

After history class, I found Miss Rasmussen waiting by the door. "I have a bone to pick with you, Gabriella. And it's serious."

"What is it?" My face grew warm.

"Aha," she said, "you feel guilty already."

"Guilty?"

"I want you in my office right after school."

"But why? What have I done?"

"It may seem like quite a small thing, but the repercussions could prove serious." She wore her white hair in a braided coronet. Her dress was a rich-looking tweed with a small velvet collar that brought the ripe apple sheen to her cheeks. To me, she was a magistrate, a ruler; I would never have done anything that would offend her. My worry must have shown in my face, for she said, "It's not too serious, Gabriella. Perhaps you haven't understood all of our rules yet, and . . . well, some of the girls have been talking."

In spite of her reassuring remark, I did worry all the rest of the day. I searched and searched my conscience looking for any wrongdoing and couldn't find a single one. I did not think that eating a chocolate kiss would merit a visit to the headmistress's office. I was wrong. When my last class had let out, I made my way to Miss Rasmussen's office in the main building. I did not know what to expect. I knew my aunt would be angry if I missed the bus and was late getting home. And what excuse could I give?

"Gabriella," Miss Rasmussen said, as she let me in and softly closed the door. "Sit down. Please."

I boosted myself into the chair and sat.

"Your teachers tell me you are doing excellent

work in all your classes. Miss Marshall tells me you are well and widely read, much in advance of the other girls."

"I do love to read," I said modestly.

"However, it is not your work that we are concerned with today. It is your social life that has gone awry, especially your friendship with Miss Plus."

"Sylvia?" I had ceased to think of Sylvia as a friend. In the days since my arrival, she had been my shelter against the storm. We had nothing in common except that we were outcasts. Nonregulation in a regulation world. Not even our uniforms could hide it.

"Indeed I do mean Sylvia. I have been told . . ." she lowered her voice ". . . that you have been buying her friendship with candy."

Through Miss Rasmussen's window, girls in blue blazers grouped and regrouped on the emerald lawns, laughing, talking, calling out good-byes. "But that's not true." My voice had dropped to the level of hers. "It's simply not true."

"I have already questioned Sylvia."

"And what did she say?"

"She said that you had been coming to school with candy from Woolworth's. She said that you had been giving her chocolate so that she would walk with you to and from the bus stop, so that she would sit with you in chapel and walk you to your next-period class."

I sat stock-still, as though I'd been struck and stunned by a hammer. I could not gather my wits to protest. "But . . . but . . . Miss Rasmussen, no, that's not how it was . . ." My thoughts were wild, that Sylvia would say that, would turn on me, accuse me of. . . . "I did have some candy, but . . ."

Miss Rasmussen rose from her desk and turned

to the window, then back. As I searched for a way to explain my innocence, she opened the cabinet beneath the sunny windows and took out a small painted watering can. "Gabriella," she said, turning to the potted geraniums, "the deed itself is not so terrible, only the implications. You see, you must realize that you cannot buy friendship. With your handicap, it would be easy to fall into the habit of buying others with the promise of reward. Any tendency to do so must be stopped at once." As she spoke, she turned each pot this way or that to give each plant its quota of water and sun.

"But, Miss Rasmussen, I didn't do that. I didn't try to buy her friendship . . ."

"Gabriella, you must not prey on the weakness of others. Sylvia has an insatiable appetite for chocolate, poor dear. Her mother has quite forbidden her to eat it." Miss Rasmussen chuckled just thinking about it. "Sylvia's condition, you know."

Bewildered and hurt, I hardly listened as Miss Rasmussen gave me further warning and dismissed me. I walked alone to the bus stop. I could scarcely believe that Sylvia had turned against me.

Tante Eloise scolded me when I got home. "Imagine it, detention already, and it's only the first month of school."

Next morning, Sylvia was not at her station, and the thought of her betraying me made me empty and cold inside. I walked alone to my first class, hobbled alone to chapel. The trees in the yard had lost all their leaves in a storm that had passed in the night, and leaves were scattered everywhere. I went inside, found my place, and tried to have a word with Him . . . if He was listening. I stood alone for singing, I sat alone for the lesson, and I knelt alone for prayer.

I didn't see Sylvia until after history. She was

strolling along, kicking up leaves—now in sunlight, now in shadow—arm in arm with Alice Boshears. Sharing her chocolate, no doubt. I could not believe that she had lied about me. I wanted to catch up to her and ask her. As I quickened my step, the taps on my shoes played a strange little offbeat tune—it could have been my theme song—which gave me away. With a toss of their heads, the two girls broke into a trot and trotted away, a feat I would not have thought Sylvia capable of. But then, I hadn't known the real Sylvia.

I wanted to faint, I wanted to die, I wanted to sprout wings and fly away like an angel. I wanted God to appear in a cloud of glory and catch me up to His bosom; and wouldn't *they* be sorry! None of this happened. I stood there like a fool and watched them go. It was at this very point that I turned vicious.

My only weapon was my mind, but black thoughts didn't hurt them. They only laughed and trotted away, laughing, talking about me behind my back. I decided I would learn everything faster and better than anyone in school. I would get the highest marks, receive the most praise; everyone would clamor to be my friend.

This didn't happen.

Every night I sat up in my basement room, poring over my books. I memorized French conjugations, tackled bilateral quadratic equations, wrote and rewrote English compositions until every word in them was perfect. I had taken the tablecloth off the carton and had spread it out on my bed as a coverlet. In between my studies, I would stare at the coverlet, at the Southern belle in her elegant gown, at her young man in his top hat and his fine cross-stitch suit, mounted on his thoroughbred, galloping through forest and flower borders to see her. I wrote a composition about it, about how someday the Southern belle would be me, how one day a handsome young man mounted on a thoroughbred hunter would pay his call.

"What imagination!" my English teacher said. "What vivid images!" She gave me an A +, but added a red pencil comment: "Perhaps you should talk to Miss Rasmussen about this."

I did not. If Rowena LeSage could have her brown-eyed young man, I could have one, too. I had entered a world of my own creation, and I would not give it up.

Tante Eloise was not happy about my new determination and began to complain that I was using too much expensive electricity in keeping my light on so late. She complained that I would make myself sick, and there would be doctors' bills. She said I would be taken away to a state institution with a fit of nerves. "And who will pay?" she demanded. "That's what I want to know."

One morning stands out in particular: She had asked me in to sit at the breakfast table in her tiny dinette, a cubbyhole that smelled of coffee and long-forgotten sausage. She had my shredded wheat and milk on the dinette table. She poured a cup of tea and asked me to sit down. "There's simply no reason for you to tax yourself so."

"I wanted you to be proud." I crossed my fingers under the table to undo this out-and-out lie. "My parents were proud when I learned to read and write. After all of your personal investment, I wanted you to reap the profits." I crumbled the biscuit into the cereal bowl, flooded it with milk, took a big spoonful, and chewed.

"Profits?" Her penciled-in eyebrows flew up. "My

34

dear Gabriella, my only hope for you is that you learn sound moral values." She sipped at her tea, winced, returned the cup to its saucer. She regarded me solemnly. "As the Good Book says, 'Lay ye not up treasures on earth where moth and mouse doth corrupt . . .' "

It was all I could do to smother my laughter.

Her cheeks grew pink. "Well . . . that quote may not be exact, but you see the wisdom in it, and that's all that counts."

A little chill ran up my spine. "I don't know what you mean."

"What I mean is very simple. What good is scholastic achievement for someone like you?" She lifted her cup to her lips, calm, composed, and told me my fate. "I don't intend to be cruel, child, but there is no place for you in this world. What hope have you but hope of heaven? Heaven must be your single pursuit."

I returned my spoon to the bowl of shredded wheat. "Excuse me, Tante Eloise, but I must start off for school. If I don't leave now I'll be late." I had added her name to the list of people I hated.

"There are crumbs on your face, Gabriella." She pushed a paper napkin across the table. "Table manners betray your station in life. Remember that, Gabriella."

"Yes, ma'am."

By that time she'd heard about Sylvia Plus and the chocolate kisses. She had yet to hear of my other misdeeds. How I tripped—yes, tripped—Alice Boshears as she passed my desk on the way to the pencil sharpener. Nor had she yet heard how I'd taken Eileen Prestrude's sack lunch from the day students' cupboard, and had substituted an identical brown paper sack containing a handful of mud and

35

a flattened water snake that I'd snatched from the gutter near the curb at my bus stop. That afternoon I'd very much enjoyed Eileen's Jonathan apple, her two chicken salad sandwiches, and her wedge of frosted angel food cake. From all the screams I heard at lunchtime I could not honestly claim that Eileen enjoyed what I'd left her. Nasty, I know. Revenge has sweet moments.

There was more to follow:

The self-same morning that Tante Eloise served up her advice along with the breakfast, I carried with me to school an accurate, if somewhat unflattering, portrait of my erstwhile friend, Sylvia. Done in Crayola on a large sheet of butcher's paper and folded to fit hidden in my notebook, the portrait brought out all of Sylvia's most salient features: her squinted eyes, her pumpkin head, her U-shaped mouth in perpetual smile, and especially her gargantuan hips, her rotund stomach, and her immeasurable tree-trunk legs. I drew her in regulation uniform, bursting at the seams. She held a large sack of Hershey's chocolate kisses, one of which she was pushing into her tiny up-turned mouth. Above the portrait, in a comic book balloon, I had written YUM! YUM!

As I was the last to leave the French room that day, nobody saw me pull out the portrait of Sylvia, unfold it, and pin it to the bulletin board, covering a dreary display of "Cultural Notes from France." My artwork proved to be a hit. It was talked about for days.

I hid books, put thumbtacks on desk seats, tossed notebooks out of third-floor windows, spilled ink on all of Miss Marshall's English composition papers—on all but mine. In chapel each morning I sang with great gusto, off-key. When I prayed, I prayed for vengeance.

\* \* \*

"Whatever are we going to do with you, Gabriella?"

I had been sent to Miss Rasmussen's office, the third time that week, and it was only Wednesday, two days to go. I sat in my customary chair, glowering, hating the world and everyone in it.

"You could shoot me," I suggested. "Line me up before a firing squad of my peers."

"Oh, my," said Miss Rasmussen, half-smiling. "Wouldn't that be rather extreme?"

"That's what they do to rebels."

"Is that what you are, Gabriella? A rebel?"

"Nobody likes me."

"Are you likable?" Her light blue eyes looked directly into mine, unswerving. "Have you tried?"

Suddenly my throat tightened. I could only nod my head a tentative yes. In spite of my firm resolve to be nasty and mean, tears stung my eyes. "I did try," I said when I could find my voice. "I tried and tried. They call me names behind my back. When I'm not looking they run up and push me. They say I'm the devil's daughter, because of my hump. But I'm not, Miss Rasmussen. I'm not."

"Of course you're not, Gabriella." Her voice was gentle, her manner kind. "People are not always at their best. All of us are full of fears, and we all have our hardships. We tend to find solace in normalcy. Anyone different from us makes us uneasy. The only answer lies in love and forgiveness. This is true for you as well as for them."

Tactfully, she passed me a box of tissues, and I took several to mop at the tears flowing down my face. "All I ever wanted was for people to like me. I didn't know it was going to be so hard."

She swiveled around in her chair to face the windows, as though the answer to the human dilemma lay somewhere past the sparkling lawns, past the volleyball nets and the chalk lines of the field hockey grounds. I waited, weeping into my wad of Kleenex. "If they're going to be mean to me," I sobbed, "I'm going to be mean right back to them."

She turned her chair to face me. "I wish I could offer some miracle, some magic that would change you into a girl like any other girl here at the academy. But I can't do that. Nor can I legislate kindness."

"All I want is a friend. Just one would do."

"I know. Friendship is our dearest help in times of trouble. It is our dearest joy in times of good fortune. As one of our greatest English poets once wrote: 'No man is an island . . .' "

"John Donne," I supplied.

Miss Rasmussen smiled. "It isn't enough to have the poets at the tip of the tongue, not if we don't take to heart the wisdom they offer. To have a friend, you must be a friend."

I recommended scowling.

"Striking out at the world will not bring you anything but pain. You can continue as you have been, playing mean tricks on the girls, or . . ." she leaned forward to look me straight in the eye, "you can change your attitude, right here, right now. Determine that you are going to enjoy life and the people around you. Nobody can make you miserable unless you let them."

"*Oh* . . . you are wrong, so very wrong! They push me, they pull my hair. They hit me on the back because they say it's good luck to touch me and then run . . ."

"Yes, yes. I am sure this is true." Light from the window made a halo of her silver hair. It pooled on the surface of her desk and made the leafy geraniums shine. "Reacting with hatred will never get you what you want, their affection. Your time here is only one phase of your journey. How do you want to spend the rest of your life? In bitterness? In hatred?" She paused to let this sink in. "Or, will you spend it in forgiveness and love, true love?"

Fine for her to say, she had none of my problems. "Can't you make them stop?"

"Perhaps. I could hand out detention slips. I could summon their parents. For every time that they hurt you I could make them suffer. But that wouldn't make them like you, now would it?"

I stared at my toes. "No," I said. "I guess not."

"The single most important thing you can learn here, Gabriella, is how to live with your hardship. It will be with you long after you have left this institution. If you like, you may come in and talk with me about your problems with the other girls. Together, we might be able to help you work things out."

"Then you're not going to send me away?"

"Of course not. You are an honor student. We are fortunate to have you here. Of course, I'm not going to send you away. What nonsense!" She got up from her chair to dismiss me.

"And you're not going to punish the others?"

"We just discussed that, Gabriella."

My mind turned in confusion; it was not fair, not fair at all. My aunt said I should live only for death. Miss Rasmussen said the others could hurt me all they wanted and get away with it. "It's not fair!" I shouted at her. "It's just not fair!"

"Good day, Gabriella."

"Good day to you, Miss Rasmussen!"

I slid out of my chair and opened her door, wishing I had the courage to slam it, kick it, smash it to

39

pieces. There was nothing I could do to express my growing rage. Hurt and angry, I turned on my heel, hurling over my shoulder a Parthian shot, *"Au revoir* to you, Miss Rasmussen!"

*"Au revoir* to you, too, Gabriella."

I stomped out of the building and down the cobblestoned walk to the bus stop. That afternoon and far into the night I used up my anger by attacking my studies with all the ferocity that was becoming second nature. I was determined, *determined*, that I, not the rest of the world, would triumph.

# 4

"Elf."

"Imp."

"Midget."

"Dwarf."

"Goblin."

"*Hob*goblin."

"That's it, *hob*goblin! Because she hobbles!"

The whole of Miss Winthrop's European history class burst into new rounds of snickers and giggles, no need to tell at whose expense. Miss Winthrop, caught up in the holiday spirit, had baked a special cake for us and had left the room to go get it. It was the end of term, just before Christmas, and all the young ladies of the academy were feeling frisky. Because I had made myself so thoroughly hated, they

41

were taking out their friskiness on me. I sat in my seat, my knees on the bolster pillow, bent over my A+ exam that Miss Winthrop had handed back before excusing herself from the classroom. I pretended to be checking for errors, knowing good and well that there were none.

"Rumpelstiltskin is her name," sang Eileen Prestrude, who excelled in music. "Care to spin your hair into gold, Rumpelstiltskin?" The room rocked with laughter.

"Be careful," cried Alice Boshears, "don't make her mad. She stomps her foot when she's mad. If she's really Rumpelstiltskin, she will stomp her foot clear through the floor."

More laughter, more raucous than ever.

Alice had plenty of reason to taunt me, as only a few days earlier, I had found her black oxfords outside her P.E. locker and had hidden them in a wastebasket so she would be late for her next class. I wanted every girl in the school to have a dose of humiliation, I wanted each of them to know exactly what humiliation felt like. I wanted them to suffer as I did.

"Question!" screamed Alice: "If Gabriella had to be one of the seven dwarfs, which one would she be?"

"That's easy," Sylvia shrieked, her face pink and quivering. As long as the others were picking on me, she and "her condition" would be relatively safe. "She'd have to be Grumpy!" Sylvia screamed at the top of her voice. "She'd have to be Grumpy, always in a frown!"

"Or Dopey!" shrieked Meg Conklin. Meg was normally a shy gentle girl, but she'd gotten caught up in the camaraderie of torture, and her piping voice shrilled like a piccolo, high above the others.

"No!" Alice cried, demanding to be heard. "Dopey's cute and lovable. He's not at all like Gabriella!"

Beneath this barrage of insults, I sat on my knees, bent over my exam paper, my face on fire, my eyes full of tears. The palms of my hands were so cold and so sweaty they left embarrassing damp spots on the varnished top of the desk.

Adrienne Twill-Smith joined the fray. She was a rough girl whose parents "had money." She had a booming voice and smoked cigarettes in the toilets. "The trouble with Gabriella," she boomed, "is she acts like she thinks she's Sleeping Beauty. But really she's the old witch. She's as nasty as a witch."

Fair enough that Adrienne should attack me: I sat behind her in French class and for the past few weeks I had fed her wrong translations when it was her turn to read before the class. Sometimes, just to keep her hopes up, I had fed her correct translations, then wrong ones again. Once, right in front of the class, she had wet her pants in her bewilderment and anguished confusion. And my voice had joined the merry laughter. It wasn't my fault that she was stupid. Now it was her turn to get back at me. "The trouble with Gabriella," she bellowed in that deep husky voice, "is she thinks she's the most!"

"But she's not the most," sweet Alice chimed in. "Sylvia's the *most*, Gabriella is the *least*!"

"She thinks she can get special treatment, just because she's little," cried Dora Van Alstein. "She thinks she can do whatever she wants to and not get punished for it. Just because she's different. She ought to get put in a home!"

"Hooray!" the group shouted as one.

"Gabriella is nothing but a mouse," Sylvia crowed, when the roar of the crowd began to die down. "She reminds me of that little comic book mouse. What's his name? What's that mouse's name?" she demanded of everyone but me.

I had never read a comic book, but I had seen other girls reading them. They brought them to school, hidden inside their spelling workbooks. Most of the comics that they read were stories of romance, with wonderful four-color covers of a man taking a woman tenderly into his arms and kissing her. The woman's thoughts were written in a balloon above her head: *"My love, my love! Oh, never leave me again, my darling!"* I had dreamed of these covers at night in my room, daydreamed about them in school.

"Sniffles!" shrieked three girls at once. "The mouse's name is Sniffles! Mary Jane and Sniffles!"

"Sniffles!" the group screamed in chorus.

At that moment, Miss Winthrop returned with the cake. By some minor miracle she did not drop it. "Sniffles?" she questioned, her eyes round and startled. "Someone in here has the sniffles?"

The room fell into an uncertain silence.

Eileen and Alice jumped up to help Miss Winthrop with the cake, easing it down on the study table in the front of the room. It was a marvelous cake, done in the shape of a medieval castle, with icing windows, drawbridge, and gate. Tiny red and green pennants flew from the turrets. I could think only of the dungeon and saw myself in it.

"Now, what is all this about sniffles?" Miss Winthrop was a tall, imposing figure, with a spectacular bosom. "I will admit it is the season for sniffles," Miss Winthrop declared, "but I see no earthly reason to make such a row about it."

The pips and squeaks of ill-suppressed laughter broke to the surface and the whole room exploded around me. In the midst of the roaring and the howling, Miss Winthrop gave me a knowing look, and when the others had gained enough control of themselves to line up at the table for a piece of castle-cake, Miss Winthrop spoke to me privately.

"You know my heart aches for you, Gabriella. But you must admit you bring your troubles on yourself, by the things you say and the things you do. You can't find love by hating, Gabriella. You will not earn respect if you do not respect others."

I clenched my jaw and turned away.

There was punch that day, too. Miss Winthrop served it from a crystal bowl that shot rainbows all around the room. The napkins were of snowy white linen with a dainty cross-stitched sprig of holly leaves and berries in one corner. The dessert plates were said to be old English china. Stories were read, poems recited, and Eileen Prestrude played a small glass xylophone that her parents had brought her from Switzerland. Calmed and content, the girls devoured the very last crumb of Miss Winthrop's cake and left only the dregs of the punch.

As for me, I did not join them.

I sat at my desk sunk in gloom. No one understood me, no one cared. I thought I'd be better off dead than to have to endure the kind of life I was living. If it hadn't been for my strong urge to live and my curiosity about what new adventure lay around the next corner, I might have given up and simply expired. As it turned out, I am glad that I lived.

# 5

Time, they say, heals all wounds. Pushed to the extreme, this may be true, I don't know. I will always be grateful that I did not have to wait out an eternity for time to heal my bitter heart.

After the Christmas holidays, the young ladies of the academy and I came to a truce: I left them alone, they left me alone. I took my place at the head of each class, and they competed among themselves for second-best. No one admired me, no one clamored to be my friend. I walked the corridors silent and alone, ate my lunch unmolested, spent weekends and the summer holiday alone in the basement. Tante Eloise brought me books from the library. When I offered to wash dishes in exchange for this kindness,

46

she sighed heavily. "Gabriella, you would only drop them and break them."

"I could learn to cook."

"You would only burn yourself."

"Let me clean the house."

"No, Gabriella, *merci bien*, but it is easier for me to do it than to have to show you how."

Tante Eloise lusted for stars in her crown.

Philosophy, psychology, geography, sciences, literature, I read them all. I do not mean to say I gained any deep understanding of these topics, but I gained a smattering of general knowledge. Academically, this placed me far ahead of the other girls who had squandered the summer in idle pursuits: swimming, going to parties, flirting . . . having fun.

I sailed through the second year at the Young Ladies' Christian Academy, in at one end, out the same way in. Egg sandwiches, shredded wheat in a bowl, and at Christmas and my birthday, a juicy dill pickle. The other girls grew tall and graceful as golden river willows; I stayed the same. Tante Eloise noted the convenience in this: there was no need to arrange for new clothes. Only Miss Rasmussen worried about my loneliness, but I would not let her come near me. I cut her dead. I was a rock.

Just before Columbus Day, in my third year at the school, my life began to change—not for the better. The week had begun in an ordinary way—with its Monday, Tuesday, Wednesday . . . but Thursday, before early dismissal, we all gathered around the hearth in Main Hall for recitations and singing.

The mantel was decorated with black paper cutouts of the Niña, the Pinta, and the Santa Maria. Miss Rasmussen made a short speech about how glad we should be about Columbus. "Except for him," she exclaimed, "we wouldn't be here." All the girls moaned and groaned, and then we sang, "O Columbia, the Gem of the Ocean," followed by a spirited tune about going to sea on a "walloping window blind," and then Alice Boshears recited, "Beyond the Blue Azores," after which I recited, "Sail On, O Ship of State," in a most dramatic fashion. I used all my different voices: a deep rumbling voice for the waves, a high excited voice for the wind, and a slow ponderous voice for the ship itself. Alice Boshears got a standing ovation. I got nothing but silence.

The bell rang, and the girls dispersed, running out to meet their parents who arrived in private automobiles to take them away to glamorous spots for the holiday. Me, I had the bus. No longer fascinated with the taps on my shoes, I hobbled along to the bus stop, imagining myself in chic high heels and silk stockings. I imagined myself on my way to meet my brown-eyed young man. I would wait beneath the willows in the Old South garden, while *he* rushed to join me on his thoroughbred hunter. He would take me away. Forever.

Pretending eased my pain, but I couldn't live my life in make-believe shoes. I climbed onto the bus, dropped in my fare. An old man shot me a frightened look, then got up and let me have his seat. As I passed him in the aisle, he reached out and touched my back to bring himself good luck. The shock of this act brought me harshly back to reality. Pretending to a life I didn't have made my true life even more painful, like after the fireworks when the rockets fall to earth and colorful explosions die away and you notice that the night is darker and colder than ever before. I felt doomed, doomed to rented rooms, doomed to charity, doomed to the fact that no one

48

would love me—ever. Alone, unloved and unlovable. Cut off.

The bus stopped at the corner near my aunt's sad house. The driver touched his cap as I struggled down the aisle with my armload of papers and books. "Please, miss . . . can I help you with that? That's quite a heavy load you've got for yourself."

"No, thank you."

"You're sure now?"

"I'm doing fine."

By the time I got home my head was aching, and my whole body felt as though I'd been physically beaten. I went down to my room, dropped the books and papers on the carton-turned-table, and fell face down upon the bed. "God . . . if You're listening, take me now. I've had it."

But he didn't.

The hours went by, who knows or cares how many, and then Tante Eloise came down the stairs to stand beneath the sixty-watt bulb. I felt her shadow fall across me like a chill. "Gabriella? Are you sick? You are, aren't you?"

I couldn't deny it.

"Oh dear . . ." She lay a cold hand on my brow. "It's all that studying, you've weakened yourself. I knew it, I just knew it. How can anyone expect me to look after you when you won't look after yourself? Things can't go on like this, I can't allow it. Something has got to be done."

She went for a thermometer, which she popped under my tongue, and, standing beneath the meek light to read it, she gave a little cry of alarm: "Oh, *mon bon Dieu!* You must go to the doctor's, and right away!"

I made some protest, and she countered with: "Don't you worry, Gabriella. I'll find the money somewhere. I've put a little by, out of Walter's insurance, and that ought to see us through. A taxi both ways, then the doctor's bill, then the medicine, and I only hope and pray you won't have to have a hospital room."

Too weak, too sick, too sad to care, I accepted her help up the stairs and waited in the parlor while she went next door to call a taxi.

The doctor was kind, as most doctors are, and had his office at the top of a long flight of stairs in an old brick building in a shabby part of town. Once in his office, I was placed on an examining table, my clothes hauled off, and I was draped in a cloth gown that opened down the back.

"Tell me," said the doctor, when he'd peered down my throat, "are you sick often?"

I shook my head.

"Have you ever seen a doctor?"

I felt about to faint. "No, never."

"Where are your parents?"

"Dead."

"Both of them?"

I nodded, and the room spun around.

He completed his examination. "I'm going to give you some medicine, Gabriella. Then I want to have a serious talk with your aunt. This medicine isn't going to taste very good, but I want you to take it faithfully four times a day until it's all gone. I will give you some different medicine to help with the pain. In five days I want to see you again. You are a very sick young woman."

A nurse came in to help me dress, for I was all in a haze. She didn't have much to say, but she regarded me with rounded eyes and seemed to be troubled by my appearance—as many people are.

He was right about the medicine not tasting good—

it was foul—but what my aunt had to tell me on the taxi ride home was worse than any bitter dose. "Gabriella . . . dear . . ." she began, "the doctor says you are in a precipitous condition. I want you to listen closely to what I have to say, for both of us will have to be brave. He says you aren't like any ordinary person who catches a cold and recovers again. He says there is not enough room in your chest for all that you have to keep in there. You are a very special person."

"Am I going to die?"

Out on the street, horns honked, buses roared by, a mounted policeman blew his whistle, children shouted, newsboys rang their cries: Life and the living flowed around us like a river.

"Oh, my dear child . . . my dear, dear child."

Tante Eloise sat stiffly on the worn plush cushion of the taxi, her blond curls covered by a blue silk scarf, her eyebrows drawn in thin red arcs above her eyes. She folded her arms across her narrow chest. " 'No man knoweth the day nor the hour . . .' "

I stared intently at her long bony face, and her eyes did not meet mine. "Then I *am* going to die."

"Gabriella, we are *all* going someday."

"But now, am I going to go now? Is that what he told you?"

"No, Gabriella, he did not. What the doctor said is that you are no longer to attend school. He says you are much too weak."

"Oh."

"Doctor says you are to move upstairs where there is more warmth and light." She sniffed. "It seems that all I have done for you has not been enough. Heaven knows, I did my best."

According to the doctor, I was to move upstairs, and I was to eat a variety of nourishing foods: puddings, milk with cream, roast beef, fish, chicken, vegetables, whole-wheat bread with butter, and a wide variety of fruits. Tante told me this and sighed. "Where will I ever find the resources? I have no vast stores of wealth, Lord knows. And you have nothing, Gabriella. Nothing."

When we arrived home, Tante Eloise prepared me a bed on the brown plush sofa in the living room, and I lay there in that luxury, such as I'd never experienced before, worried and fearful about what would become of me. I had nearly finished my work at the academy. I hated to leave there before it was done, but worse . . . how would I live? My aunt prepared a lovely blancmange with eggs and cream and sugar, so fragrant with vanilla it could have descended straight from heaven, but I could not eat a single spoonful. I could see by the set of her jaw that she had something more to tell me, and it would not be good.

"Gabriella," she began, "this isn't easy."

I lay very still beneath the blanket, a wave of cold creeping over my skin. I stared at a figure in the carpet and waited.

"Gabriella . . . I will no longer be able to keep you."

I nodded to show I understood.

"As soon as you are stronger, we must look for more suitable arrangements." She focused on a point in the middle distance, somewhere between a wing-back chair and the lace curtains that draped the sunny window. "You know how it is, dear. I can't afford to feed you all the expensive food that the doctor demands for you. And the bills . . . the medicines . . . you do understand. Tell me you do, Gabriella."

"Yes." I couldn't raise my voice above a whisper. "You have been kind."

She patted my arm, and her manner became almost lively. "Now don't you worry, always remember the Lord will provide. If He cares for the smallest sparrow, how could He forget us, His children? And did He forget Noah in the time of the floods? Or Daniel in the lion's den? Or the Hebrew prophets in the fiery furnace? Or . . . ?"

My mind turned to Peter upside down on his cross, to Stephen stoned to death, to Congo missionaries with their heads ripped off in the name of the Lord, and I did not care to join them. As to sparrows, I had encountered innumerable storm-battered sparrows dead in the streets. If He was keeping an eye on them, what did He watch them do? With a quick little step that could have been a dance step, Tante Eloise went back to the kitchen with the uneaten portion of blancmange, leaving me alone to worry, then sleep.

Upon my return visit to the doctor, he told me that I would have to learn to use crutches. "As you grow stronger," he said, then corrected himself, "*if* you grow stronger, and with plenty of sunshine, a good diet, plenty of strengthening exercise, you might . . . someday . . . you might be able to put the crutches aside."

"Doctor . . . ?" I had something to ask him, something I hated to ask him, something I simply had to ask him, but I was afraid of the answer. I was sitting in the awkward gown, on the examining table.

"Yes?" He had steely blue eyes that looked straight at me.

"Doctor . . . is there anything that will make me grow?" I turned away. I couldn't look at him for just a moment, and then when I did I wished I hadn't. Sad and still, in that dingy office with its stacks of folders and papers, its shelves of dusty medical books, its tattered window blinds, and with the medical skeleton hanging from its steel frame, grinning at us, its bones all numbered and labeled, its soul long gone out the window, the doctor turned away to study his hands, as if to measure their capacity for healing, their capacity for making me normal. He shook his head, and my heart fell.

"I'm sorry to say, Gabriella, that it simply isn't possible."

"There's nothing? No medicine? An operation, maybe? I'd take any kind of shot. I'm very brave. I'm not afraid of needles. I'll do anything. *Anything*."

"We're talking about your body, Gabriella. There is nothing in our medical books that will make your body grow. But there's no limit to how high your spirit can grow. You're very bright: Use your mind, develop it. You'll never know what you can do until you try."

This was not what I wanted to hear.

"I'm sorry, Gabriella. That's all I can offer."

He opened a door in the wall behind his cluttered desk, revealing a storeroom. It seemed a dark cavernous place, giving off a musty smell, with vials and test tubes and boxes of mysterious-looking bottles arranged on shelves, shrouded wheelchairs, and stacks of chipped enamel bedpans, one of which clattered to the floor as the doctor pushed his way into the room and turned on the light. "Ah . . ." He dug through a collection of canes and crutches, tossing one after another aside until at last he found what he was searching for, a pair of wooden crutches shorter than all the others. "These should do." He turned back to me, eyed me critically, eyed the crutches. "Yes, let's try these." He switched off the light and closed the door. "Here, Gabriella, I'll show you how

54

to use them. Let's hope they bring you better fortune than they brought their previous owner."

Fortunately for me, the crutches were the perfect length.

I did not ask to hear the story of their previous owner, and the doctor did not volunteer it. He showed me how to tuck them beneath my armpits, how to support my weight, how to swing my legs forward, swing the crutches forward, and start again. Up and down the black rubber runner in the dim hallway we went, with Tante Eloise looking on through teary eyes. The weakness in my legs had made me a cripple, a pitiful creature, helpless. How I hated the look on her face.

When I'd mastered the fundamentals of my new mode of locomotion, the doctor and I said good-bye. He asked me to write to let him know how I was getting on, and I promised I would, knowing full well I would not.

Out on the street my aunt bought several newspapers, some local, some from far away. "We'll study the ads," she said. "I don't want to send you to an institution, Gabriella. But that will be our only choice, unless we can find you some type of employment. But who would hire you? And for what? Don't get your hopes too high, *ma chérie*. Your chances at best are slim."

At that point, I had no hopes at all.

We took a taxi home and pored over all the papers, circling ads that looked at all promising: a mother's helper, a companion to an elderly lady in a wheelchair, and an opening for a chore girl on a farm. After a nourishing supper, for which I had no appetite, I sat at the table in the dinette and composed letters of application. I paid particular attention to spelling and punctuation. I used my very best penmanship, my aunt's best stationery, her best pen and ink. I was earnest, I was cheerful, I was dependable; I was completely correct. I was desperate.

The mother with the children didn't answer. Days after I'd sent my letters off, I received a purple envelope containing a lavender-scented note: "Old Alice died yesterday. Thanks, anyway." And ten days after that, when I was completely disheartened, certain that I would find no employment and certain that my loving tante would put me in an institution, a letter arrived from the farm, postmarked Montana.

Deer Mz. Wheeler,
I'm plizzed to inform you that you kan come by Tran and my son and Myseff wil bee plizzed to meet you. An Mama too. If it not be too kold for her. You mzt wurk hard an not git intoo no truble. You kno what I min?
Hmbly Yrs.
Joseph P. Shevala.

Tante Eloise took on a sheen of ecstasy. "This is wonderful news, Gabriella! I shall go right now down to the railroad depot and arrange for schedules and a ticket for you. Then you must write directly back to give your employer the particulars of your arrival. This is a chance in a lifetime, Gabriella. It's exactly what we have been waiting for."

So much to do: pack my books, pack my few articles of clothing, write the letter, make arrangements. I had earlier arranged to take the GED to get my high school diploma and had no intention of letting this go. During the last few days at my aunt's house, I sat upstairs in any of a number of comfortable chairs, in a sunny window seat, on the sofa, and studied for my exam. I had made up my mind

56

to have my diploma and was not going to leave for the West without it. On the day of the test I arrived at the appointed station, pencil in hand and a stomach full of butterflies. But the test was simple and I passed with flying colors.

With this victory to keep me strong, I was able to rise early the morning of my departure, bathe, dress, and have myself ready by the time my aunt was ready to leave. We took a taxi to the depot, I remember, and I remember my sense of growing terror, as Tante helped me find the right platform and handed me a brown paper sack containing my chopped egg sandwiches, which she had made for me the night before.

"Do you have your ticket, Gabriella?"

"I've got it."

"Are you certain, Gabriella?" She dabbed at her eyes with her hanky.

I stood with my crutches tucked beneath my arms, dug the ticket out of my pocket, and showed it to her. My mouth was dry and my throat felt so tight I couldn't trust myself to speak.

"You know how badly I feel about this, don't you, Gabriella?"

"*Yes.*" I couldn't speak above a whisper. I didn't want her to know how scared I was, that I didn't want to go, that I wanted to go back, that I would be willing to spend the rest of my life in the basement, that I would do whatever she asked if *only* she would let me return. I didn't want to make this journey, couldn't make it, wouldn't make it; I refused.

"You know I'd give anything, *anything,* if I could afford to keep you, Gabriella." She sniffed, touched her nose with the lace of her hanky, then went on to hand me a last nugget of wisdom: "Remember this, and never forget, 'The wind is tempered to the shorn lamb.' Which means, *ma fille*, that you will never be asked to bear more than you can.' "

"*Merci beaucoup.*"

"Farewell, my dearest. *Ma chère* Gabriella, *adieu!*"

Because of the awkwardness of my crutches, she made no attempt to embrace me, and I was grateful. The conductor helped me up the steps and through the door and helped me find my seat by a window. I can see my aunt now, waving from that early morning platform. I do not recall waving back.

When I settled myself and my crutches I felt a sudden fit of terror and willed my soul to my maker. As the engine built power, as iron wheels shuddered and squealed beneath the floor, vast clouds of pinkish-colored steam rose and flattened against the window, blotting out everything I'd ever known. My aunt was gone, the city was gone, my past was gone.

First came terror, then denial of terror. I had the strangest sense that I was floating free of my body, as if some urgent life's prayer had just been answered. I felt free, not only free from the circumstances of a life I deplored, but I felt as though I'd been freed from this bone, this skin, this shape that had contained me, contained me like a prison.

Out West I'd be somebody new; I wouldn't have to be me anymore. The Scriptures had always made this vague promise of renewal, of putting off the old self and putting on the new, but until that single shining moment when the train first shuddered and squealed and started to move forward in short arthritic jerks, I had not believed that the promise in the Scriptures could ever apply to me. My imagination caught fire, soared: I would live the life I'd been meant to live—gracious surroundings, gentle companions, philanthropic thoughts. Any family rich enough to own a whole farm—a whole farm!—and to take on servants as carelessly as they were taking me on, that family would have to be wealthy, and to wealthy I added well-bred, Mr. Shevala's spelling notwithstanding. I imagined the Old South, as I'd seen it done in cross-stitch in my mother's tablecloth: stately gardens, acres of rolling green, hunt scenes with foxes and hounds, and me in my picture hat strolling among the willows.

Oh, but they were going to be sorry . . . that Sylvia, that Eileen, that Alice Boshears, all of them. Oh, they would write me, letter after letter, to apologize. But would I find the time to write them back? Hardly. I might send a snapshot of me and my new life. A newsletter to the school, at Christmastime, that might be nice. Pictures of me and my horses, of me and my beaux, of me and my brown-eyed young man, and I, like the seductive Rowena LeSage, would be smiling . . . slightly. Just a hint of mystery, a dash of satisfaction.

"God," I prayed, "look after me now. And while You're at it, could You find someone to care about me? Please? No, *make* somebody care about me. If You are all they say You are, if You can manufacture eternity in the twinkling of an eye, then surely . . . *surely* . . . You can do this one simple thing for me. I'm not choosy. Anyone at all will do."

No sooner had I said this than a large gentleman with whiskey breath and thick leather boots lurched and fell heavily into the seat next to mine. Half an inch more and he would have crushed me. The cuffs of his shirt were dirty and frayed, his nose was red, and he smelled bad. I shut my eyes tight to add a single word of postscript: *"Him???"*

Happily, my seatmate hadn't a jot of romantic interest in me. He pulled his hat low and soon started

59

up a sonorous snoring. I moved away as far as I could, determined to keep his arms, legs, and elbows from touching any part of mine.

I soon realized that unless I were to climb onto my knees, I wouldn't be able to see much through the window except steam, and behind the steam, nightmare shadows of smokestacks, spires, and rooftops as the train crossed through the city. When the sun appeared and the steam rolled away, I caught sight of blue sky and now and then a wooded hillside rose into view. We had left the city behind, and I wanted very much to see the countryside, yet I was intimidated by the man snoring away beside me, and I could only guess at barnyards, at cattle knee-deep in a silver stream, at freckle-faced children waving from a berry patch and wishing they were on the train with me. Soon the porter came swaying down the aisle, seeing to passengers' comfort. He was a small supple black man dressed in a dark blue suit with brass buttons, a funny round cap that made him look like a peddler's monkey, polished black shoes. He stopped at my seat, smiled in a pleasant way, and pulled the window shade down to keep out the sun. He touched his cap in a kind of salute, but I was too shy to know how to respond.

I had worn my school jumper and blazer, and my regulation socks kept falling down. Tante Eloise had insisted that I take along my horrible coat, saying, "I've heard it gets remarkably cold out west."

So I had taken the coat, just to be polite, and had allowed the conductor to dispose of it on the luggage rack high overhead. As far as I was concerned, that was the end of the hideous thing: R.I.P.

As the train rattled on through the bright afternoon and on through the colors of evening, the person that I'd always been grew smaller with distance.

I'd been given a second chance, granted a reprieve. Out west I'd do everything better, be a better person, make my own way. Everyone would love me out west. Over trestle, through dark and roaring tunnel, past clusters of towns that glittered like jewel boxes against the dark velvet of night, I found hope once again. My life would be different in Montana.

# 6

Late that night we arrived in Chicago, where I had to change trains. My aunt had explained the procedure, as much as she knew, from having questioned the stationmaster back in St. Louis. "It's simple," she'd said. "Disembark from the train that you're on, walk a short distance to a central information area, ask for the platform number of the train that is printed on your ticket. Anyone there can help you." She pinned me with her eyes. "Have you got that straight?"

Now, with the train pulling into Chicago, I wished I'd paid stricter attention to my aunt's instructions. The train slowed down, the coach lights came on, and there commenced a general commotion of passengers and trainmen. I felt my heart begin to pound. My breath came in short quick gasps.

Fears like demons assailed me: I would lose my ticket, I would stumble and fall and be trampled to death. I would not find the stairs leading up to the El that Tante Eloise had told me about. I had to go out of the station, find the El, climb the long flight of stairs in the dark and the rain, then find the right station to catch the train for Montana. I'd be late, I knew it, and the train for Montana would leave without me, and I'd die in the slums of Chicago, broken and betrayed, like one of the miserable dogs out of *Beautiful Joe.*

I'd deliberately left my egg sandwich lunch under the seat, and I was planning to leave my horrible coat on the overhead rack for any unfortunate who might want to claim it; I would have only myself and my crutches to worry about. Excited, scared, almost sick, I waited for the train to come to a halt and for the doors to open on Chicago.

The gentleman in the seat next to mine had slept through most of the trip, waking only now and then for a lurching lopsided journey toward the toilets, or toward the dining car, or more often toward the lounge car, where, as the poets say, ". . . he had drunk his fill." He had scarcely even noticed me, for which I was thankful. As the train bumped, thumped, and finally shrilled to a stop, this same man got to his feet and snapped his fingers for the porter. "Get my coat, boy."

"This be your coat, sir?"

To my horror, the porter hauled down my own ill-fitting charity-box garment.

"Nope," replied my seatmate. "That's none of mine."

"How about you, little lady? Could this be yours?"

"Nope," I answered with a cool equivalence, "it's none of mine, either."

The porter and my seatmate grinned at each other, and my seatmate handed the porter some coins. "My overcoat and luggage, boy. Hear me?"

In my struggle to get out of my seat and out into the aisle, I dropped a crutch, which clattered to the floor and slid beneath the forward seat. My seatmate, his overcoat over his shoulders, his suitcase now in hand, slipped into the stream of disembarking passengers, and the porter moved along, unaware of my dilemma.

I tugged and pulled but could not dislodge the crutch. If I pulled it forward, the shoulder part got stuck beneath my seat, and when I pushed it the other way, the end got caught beneath the footrest of the forward seat. I was afraid I'd miss the next train. I didn't want to spend the rest of my life behind some ashcan in Chicago, yet I couldn't get very far without both crutches.

It was then that I heard *his* voice for the very first time. Smooth and golden as sweet clover honey, the voice said, "Hello. May I help you with that?"

I looked straight up and into the face of my brown-eyed young man. Brown shoes, brown trousers, brown jacket, brown vest, and a white boiled shirt like the shirts my father always wore to his job at the bank. He wore a dark blue tie with small green Scotty dogs patterned on it. Over his arm he carried a tweed overcoat, which put me in mind of country things: farm breakfasts with biscuits, roosters crowing at dawn, weather vanes, storms, harvests, and wagons breaking down.

"Oh, my," I said, "yes. Yes, you may."

"Let's see . . ." Black brows drew up in a puzzled

frown. "Here . . ." he murmured, tackling the crutch from a different angle, his arm casually brushing up against mine. "Excuse me . . . did I bump you? I'm sorry."

"Oh, no . . . no . . . that's quite all right. Sorry to be a bother to you." I stole another glance at his face so close to mine, at his teeth as white and square as Chiclets. I could have stayed that way the rest of the night, so close, feeling his warmth, inhaling his fragrance. Except that the coach car had emptied.

"There," he said, brushing against me once more, "I've almost got it."

Unlike the other men on the train, he was not wearing a hat. His straight brown hair came down to his collar, which made me think that he could have been an artist, maybe, or a poet.

"Cast your worries aside." He held up my freed crutch, victorious.

I could not trust myself to speak, I was so shaken.

"Let's go," he said, with a note of authority, yet kindly, too. "I'll see that the brakeman holds your train."

He did as he'd promised and was soon out the door and into the night, hurrying away bareheaded, though the weather in Chicago was cold that night, and rainy.

The brakeman lifted me down to the platform, crutches and all, in one long swoop.

"Now where you going to, little lady?" he asked.

"Out west."

"Out west?" He laughed in open amusement. "How is it that a cute little gal like you is going out west? Those wild Indians catch you, they'll scalp you. They'll give you a haircut for free. That's how they do things out west." He winked at the gray-haired conductor who stood at the door checking tickets and holding back the crowd of people waiting to board.

The strangeness of everything made me shiver as much as the cold. I summoned up courage to ask my question, but the porter was too busy teasing me, and I couldn't get a word in edgewise. ". . . and cowboys," he was saying, ". . . you've got to look out for those cowboys . . . and the mustangs . . ."

The old conductor patted my shoulder. "Don't put any stock in that fibber. Out west is no different from anyplace else, except that there's so much of it that there's lots more room for a person to grow." He said this in all apparent seriousness, not in any mocking or unkind way. It was as if he believed that I would grow, that it was possible.

With a rush of gratitude I thanked him for his comments and asked him to direct me to the El.

"This is nasty weather for you to be out in. And you've got a long cold climb ahead of you. Be careful, now. The wind is fearsome."

With some reluctance he showed me the way. In spite of the rain, the air smelled foul, like blood, death, slaughter. I hunched into the rain, head down, and swung along on my crutches, moving at a determined pace. I wasn't accustomed yet to crutches, and the part that went under my armpits had rubbed against the tender flesh, and my hands were blistered from gripping the wood. I grew tired very quickly, but the crowd kept pushing against me so I couldn't stop to catch my breath or get my bearings. High overhead on tracks made invisible by storm and darkness, a train hurtled by, more like a ghost train than a transport for the living. I saw human faces in the windows of the brightly lighted dining car, a blur of white linens, waiters bearing silver trays, and then they were gone. So many people I'd had no idea the world could hold so many people. And there were more trains, more windows full of faces, more souls rushing onward to nameless destinations. Trains full of people shattered the night with their roar. Iron wheels racketing down steel tracks sent cinders in rose-red bouquets to spark against the foul black atmosphere before they fell in the form of grit and ash, like shrouds, across the crowds of people on the platforms, across the crowds still looking for their stations.

So many people; they bumped against me as if I were a lamppost. Pushed this way, shoved that way, I could hardly keep my balance on the slippery cement, while overhead speeding trains with their red-devil eyes blasted my ears with their screams. Battered, driven, blinded, I stumbled into a doorway that smelled fiercely of whiskey and vomit. My body shook with pain, my thoughts were all confusion. I couldn't go on. I was lost.

When I stared into the crowd, it was all legs and suitcases, blurred by the drenching rain. One figure looked familiar: thick leather boots, overcoat, battered black suitcase. It was my seatmate from St. Louis. He would help me, surely. Desperate to reach him before he disappeared, I hurried out into the tangle of legs and luggage, struggling not to slip and fall, pushing myself forward, finding myself a space in the stream. I tried to call out but there was too much noise for him to hear me. But if only I could catch up to him, maybe I could walk beside him and he would be my buffer against the crowds, and if I asked him, surely he would help me find my platform and I wouldn't miss my train. Was this too much to ask of a fellow human being?

Apparently.

The wind had increased so that it blew hard and cold at my back. My former seatmate stopped beneath a streetlamp to light a cigarette, and I raised one crutch to catch his attention. His match flared orange and went out. He lifted his head and looked at me. I smiled and waved, then hurried toward him, as he pushed through the crowds to get to me. He didn't return my smile until the moment we met, then he gave me an ugly leer, reached out with one arm, and struck me—struck me!

He didn't strike from anger, I know that now, nor did he strike out of malice. What he did, he did strictly for his own profit: touch a hunchback, and the world is your oyster. Strike a dwarf, and give the devil his due. Dumbly, ringing with shock and pain, the wind at my back as bitter as my heart, I stood there in the falling rain, as he slipped back into the flowing stream of humanity and glided away.

Out of that black moment a miracle appeared. Or was it a miracle? Some would claim it was mere coincidence that my brown-eyed young man came forward out of the crowd, found me standing there battered, shocked in body and mind, my garments soaked through, chilled heart and soul by what had just happened. Could I believe it was an answer to my prayers that *he* was on his way west, too?

Without a word, he lay an arm lightly across my shoulders, like a shield, and gently, gently, guided me through the crowds, sending his warmth throughout my whole body. Together we found the right flight of stairs, together we climbed them, one by one, in spite of the wind and the driving rain. "May I see your ticket?" he asked. "I would like to see you safely on board."

I felt a warm glow, as if a lantern had been set down inside me. "You are very kind."

"My pleasure."

68

He saw me safely to the proper car of the proper train, tactfully helping me up the steps and through the heavy train doors, and then he waited as I settled myself in my assigned seat in the parlor car. I had never imagined such luxury as now surrounded me, everything posh and plush and trimmed with gold, yet it seemed exactly right, because I was there with him. My heart was bursting with feeling, but I couldn't speak for fear of giving up my secret: that I had dreamed of him, only of him, for as long as I could remember.

When he was certain that I was comfortable, he reached into a pocket of his suitcoat for a wallet, from which he took out an embossed calling card. "If you ever need anything, someone to talk to, any help of any kind, please get in touch with me."

"I will."

"Promise?"

"I promise."

He smiled as if we already shared some wonderful secret. "Don't forget."

As if I ever could.

He wished me good luck on my journey, then moved along with the rest of the boarding passengers. I was in such a glow I couldn't read the card he had given me, but I held it tightly as if it were the token sign that my prayers had been listened to, and heeded. There were crystal chandeliers in the parlor car; prisms of crystal scattered rainbows all around as the bright light struck them, which made me think of Noah and the ark, how the Lord had set a rainbow in the sky to remind Noah and all of Noah's descendants that the Lord really loved them, in spite of everything.

The train had fallen into a comforting rhythm and

was long out of the city before I was able to examine the card that my brown-eyed young man had handed me. I read it again and again.

---

475 Last Chance Gulch, Helena, Montana

TIMOTHY G. BRENTWOOD
Minister of the Lord
Healing Hands
Riverside Church of the Brethren

---

I fell into a warm and drowsy sleep, still holding the calling card. At some dark hour of the night, the porter came by with a plump white pillow for my head and a blanket to cover me, and I still held the card tightly in my fingers, as if there were some danger that it might fly away and my brown-eyed young man would be lost to me forever.

# 6

"Whitefish!"

"*White* . . . fish!"

"Whitefish, Montana!"

The conductor's cries broke into my dreams, but I couldn't wake myself until I felt his hand on my shoulder, shaking me gently. "Come on along now, time to rise and shine. If you don't get a move on, we might just carry you on to Seattle!"

With a groan, I pulled my blanket up over my face, pretending I'd gone back to sleep. When I was certain he had gone, I sat up and looked around. The train was rushing along at the same speed as ever, with no indication that it ever meant to stop. Except for the aisle lights, the car was dark, and very warm. I climbed onto my knees to look out the window.

The bleakest scenes of winter met my eyes. A clouded moon rode high above a ragged black forest; a field of snow sprang into view and out again; pine trees glittered over frozen rivers, a farmhouse with lighted windows, a fenceline deep in snow. Snow on rooftops, snow on barns, drifts of snow, banks of snow piled almost to the height of the train. We roared through a tunnel and came roaring out the other side, where a white deer stood alone and strange on a hillock of blue-shadowed snow, and we roared onward, leaving it behind.

I felt the clutch of panic at my throat: we were almost there. Would I really be different, or would I be the same?

I grabbed up my crutches, thrust them under my arms, and made my way toward the ladies'. Inside, the room smelled of face powder, cigarette smoke, stale perfume. Worse, it reeked of truth. Until that moment I had managed to avoid looking into mirrors, full-length mirrors. I'd studied my face, my hair, my eyes in hand mirrors but I'd never been able to face the truth. But there it was, bolted to the wall beside the line of sinks: the sight that I'd spent my energies trying to deny . . . monster-me.

This creature confronted me stripped of all pretending: no-color eyes grown wide with what they saw; the face gray as ash, thin lips turned blue and beginning to tremble, witch's wiry hair like a tangle of snakes, broad shoulders, long arms reaching nearly to the floor, legs like matchsticks scarcely held me up. The uniform was wrinkled, my socks falling down. A zoo should have housed me, that's where I belonged. Come and feed the animals. Come and feed the freaks.

72

What would these farm people make of me? They'd have one good look at what they'd taken on and send me back. Send me back to what? Tante Eloise? An institution? I'd rather die. I thought of knives, ropes, poison, but nothing was at hand. I might have drowned myself in the toilet if there hadn't been a loud knocking at the door. "Better hurry up, little missy. We don't stop long at this station."

I threw myself against the heavy door to open it. Tears were pouring down my face, but the porter tactfully ignored them. "You got all you taking with you?" he asked.

"Yes."

"Where be your coat?"

"I don't need a coat."

"Don't need no coat, hunh?"

"I don't notice the cold." I pushed by him, swinging my crutches down the aisle, tears flooding my cheeks and dripping off my chin.

I arrived at my seat, the porter close behind me.

"You don't notice the cold, you special or something?"

As if he didn't *know*, as if he couldn't *see*, what I was. "Yes, I'm special," I snapped, and mopped at my chin. "I'm very special, you simply can't get more special than me."

"Hunh," he shrugged, unimpressed. "I'm pretty special, too, but you won't catch me running out in this weather, catching my death, making good Christian folks worry."

Ignoring these remarks, I turned my attention to straightening my jumper, retying my shoes, pulling my socks up, blowing my nose. By the time the train had come to its stop, the porter was there to see me through the heavy doors of the parlor car, and I had my first frigid taste of the West.

"You got folks here to meet you, little miss?"

"Yes. Thank you."

"I don't see anyone looking around for you."

"They'll be here," I insisted. "They'll be here, they promised."

He had put on a warm-looking jacket of dark brown leather, the color of his face and hands. His breath came out in stiff little clouds, like smoke. He held me to steady me, and before I realized what he was doing, he had taken his jacket off and was slipping it over my shoulders.

"Oh, *no* . . . I can't take your jacket."

"Don't you fret about taking the jacket. This here's not strictly my jacket, it got left behind and wasn't nobody wanted to claim it."

Cold gripped my lungs and without another word I accepted the jacket. Without it I would have perished, I know it.

From the door of the parlor car, the conductor called down, "Best of everything to you, little lady!"

"Best of it all to you, too!" I called back.

The porter had disappeared inside the train. It was early morning, just before dawn, and though I peered through the falling snow, I hadn't seen anyone who could have been Joseph Shevala. The stationmaster helped me find my suitcase and box of books, but there was a worried expression on his broad stubbled face, and he kept looking at the pocket watch he carried on a golden chain. "We don't hold the station open for this early morning traffic, miss. I hope you have someone coming to meet you."

"I have." I waited nonchalantly, whistling to show my unconcern, studying the hustle and bustle of trainmen as the train increased its power, roaring and squealing where it waited on the tracks. How I wished I could sneak back on board and go with it wherever it went. Children were crying, voices calling . . . good-bye, good-bye. When I caught sight of *him*, Timothy, I felt as though I'd stepped off into space. I was sure he hadn't seen me, but I watched as he got into a car full of friends. The car door slammed, and he was gone in a roar of exhaust. My heart was pounding so loudly in my ears I hardly noticed the last "Alla Board!" The train blasted, roared, jerked itself forward, and with a great rush of noise pulled out of the station. So much for love and adventure, I found myself standing alone on the deserted platform, freezing. Even the porter's jacket wasn't enough to protect me from that arctic cold.

What if it had been a joke?

I thought of Jack London and his stories of the North, where people froze to death on every page, apparently without too much discomfort. A little pain in the extremities . . . a little drowsiness . . . and one could pass gracefully away not to be discovered until snow melted in the spring.

It was then I heard the first clear shout: "Gabriella? *Gab-ri-ell-a-a-a?*" He stretched the name out.

I saw him coming toward me from the far end of the station platform, a tall man in a greatcoat that swung wide about the tops of his high leather boots. "Anyone here answer to Gabriella?" he shouted, though I was the only soul there. "I'm looking for a Gabriella Harriet Wheeler!"

Startled by his appearance, I didn't answer right away. He approached in his long rapid stride, moving through the scrim of falling snow. Swarthy complexion, dark slanted eyes, and a tall fur hat—a Cossack's hat—could not have belonged to the man who had placed an ad in the paper for a chore girl. He belonged to a gypsy camp, with firelight dancing around him.

"I'm afraid," I said, "that you must be looking for me."

Standing in the lamplight, he cast a giant shadow. "For you?" he demanded, his amazement equal to my own. "You are Gabriella Harriet Wheeler? You are a chore girl?"

"I am." As one would do in the presence of any wild animal, I stood very still and let him come up to me.

A second man, younger and slimmer than the first, though just as swarthy, appeared out of the darkness to stand within the lamplight. A tracery of mustache gave him an arrogance the older man did not possess. Snowflakes clung to his black fur hat. "So?" he demanded. "Is this it? Is this what we've come out in the cold to collect? Is this your present for Mama?"

The older man put out his hand. "I am Joseph Shevala. And this . . ." he jerked his head to indicate the younger man ". . . is my no-good son, Ambrose."

I gave him my hand. "How do you do?"

Ambrose gave me a sullen stare.

The older Shevala heaved a sigh of grief. "See?" he said, turning his dark eyes on my face. "See what I have to put up with?"

"Old fool," Ambrose muttered.

His father raised an arm as if to strike him, but then didn't. He looked down on me and scowled. His appearance was so imposing I forgot about the terrible cold. "You never said you were such a little person. I don't know if you can be useful to Mama. Tell me . . . can you milk a cow?"

"Yes." I pulled my jacket about me, but it did little good.

"How many?" he demanded. His dark eyes glared. "Come on, speak up."

I had never seen a living cow, but I had read about them, and they had never seemed to be difficult creatures. "If I have to, I can milk the whole herd."

"Chickens?"

"Chickens, too."

"Tell me, little woman, what do you know about chickens?"

My closest adventures with chickens had been limited to those occasions when a feather worked its way out of a pillow, and for lack of anything better to do, I had turned it around and had worked it back into the pillow. "I know all it is wise to know about chickens."

The tone grew more gruff. "Cook?" he shouted. "Can you cook?"

The train had gone, the station house was locked and empty. "I can cook anything you bring me."

"Clean?"

"Whatever is dirty."

He threw back his head and roared in his great booming laughter. "Horses?" he roared. "Can you shoe horses?"

"I can shoe them, every foot."

"Plow?"

"In any direction."

He slapped the silent Ambrose on the back. "Hear that, silly boy, bane of my existence? Now, what do you think of my present for Mama?"

Ambrose gave me a scalding look. "If we keep standing here, we'll freeze to death. I'm afraid this *present* you've ordered is going to scare the horses. I'll bring them around, but it's a good thing they're both wearing blinders."

The son's disrespect did nothing to dampen his father's spirits. Hands on hips, his arms akimbo, and with his greatcoat flapping like the wings of strong birds, he searched around for questions to test me. "Children? What do you know about children?"

"Some grow up," I hurled back, unthinking. "Some die, and some stay children forever."

My questioner hooted with pleasure. "Ambrose! Hey-you, Ambrose! Listen to what we've got here. It's not just a chore girl we'll take home to Mama, it's philosophy! Hear me, Ambrose? She speaks philosophy!" He shouted this into the darkness beyond the lighted platform, his head and shoulders feathered white with snow. He gazed down on me with respect, but I could think only of the wagon and hoped it would be warm. "Ah . . ." he said, "yes . . . you are deep, little woman. You're a thinker." He sighed again and looked down at my suitcase and carton of books. "These yours?"

"Wait, they're heavy . . ."

But he had already hoisted the carton onto one shoulder and had tucked the suitcase beneath his free arm as if they weighed nothing at all. "I can hardly wait to show you to Mama. Oh, but she's going to be pleased."

I followed him across the icy planks of the platform to where Ambrose waited with wagon and team. When the older Shevala had settled my possessions in the back of the wagon, he turned to help me in, clucking over me, exclaiming that I might hurt myself. He made me a place on a thick bearskin rug behind the wooden seat where Ambrose sat muttering and cursing. "There," he said, tucking a fleecy warm quilt around me, "are you ready, little one?"

"Quite ready, Mr. Shevala."

"Papa Joe," he said, as he settled himself on the bearskin beside me. "You should call me Papa Joe, like everyone else."

On the wagon seat, Ambrose snorted. "Crazy Joe,

that's what they call you, crazy old Gypsy Joe." He slapped the long reins against the backs of the horses, and with a jingling of harness the wagon moved forward into the bitter darkness. If it hadn't been for the whiteness of the snow, the horses could never have found their footing on the icebound road we were to take, and even so they slipped from time to time and the wagon lurched from one side to the other.

At one such moment, the wagon jerked sharply to the left, and I threw my arms to the side to catch my balance. Papa Joe caught me. "Be careful, you must look out for the stove."

Until then I hadn't even noticed the so-called "stove," for I was still in shock from what I'd encountered, the strangeness not only of the landscape but also my employer.

"Here, little woman. Beneath the driver's seat, see it? We heat up bricks in an old iron bucket and we set the bucket under Ambrose, to sweeten his sour disposition." Papa Joe hooted at his private joke, then, gaining control, explained, "This is our way, the Bohemian way, of building a traveler's stove. Only take care not to touch it, or you will get yourself a burn. Throws out heat like the fires of hell, hot bricks in a bucket."

"It is very warm," I admitted.

In spite of the bearskin, the quilt, and the bucket, my flesh felt chilled to the bone, and I doubted I would ever get warm again. "Bohemians must be very ingenious people, Mr. Shevala."

"What is this, *Mister* Shevala?"

"I meant Papa Joe."

The gruff voice gentled. "That's what they call me up here in this country."

Dark as a phantom on the buckboard seat, Ambrose made a noise of ultimate crudeness. "Dumb *Bohunk*, that's what they call you, *Bohunk*."

Papa Joe sprang to his feet. "Bohunk, is it? That's what you call your father, the man who sired you, you worthless get. Bohunk, is it? Bohunk?"

Ambrose cleared his throat and spat over the side of the wagon. "If the shoe fits . . ."

I cowered against the side panel of the wagon, certain there would be violence, but suddenly the older man changed his tune. "Didn't you hear our little Gabriella? She said Bohemians are a genius people. She's not like you, my dearest son, she is intelligent. She reads books. She comes from the city, where people know things and can talk about them."

"She didn't say genius," Ambrose said.

"She did. She said genius. Didn't you, little woman? You said genius, I heard you. Clear as a bell, I heard you." Standing up on the wagon bed, he towered so high above me that it seemed as though the new stars of morning had clustered on his hat. "Speak up, little treasure. Tell us again what you said."

"Ingenious. I said, 'Bohemians are very ingenious.' "

"See there!" cried Papa Joe.

"She said *in*-genius."

"*In*-genius, *out*-genius. What does it matter? Another word out of you, and I'll give you a crack alongside the head."

Ambrose said nothing more, for the moment.

"Hurry those horses," Papa Joe commanded. "I want to get our treasure home to Mama."

"Treasure?" Ambrose spat into the dark. "Let's throw her out, leave her in the ditch. Some kind of treasure, little stunted dwarf girl. She belongs in a circus, not on a farm. Mama needs help with the house and the children, not another mouth to feed, one more thing for her to have to worry about. If this woman's a treasure, I'm a pig's hind end."

Papa Joe's laughter rang out against the dark and the cold. "Well and truthfully spoken, my son. Truthfully, spoken very well." Darker than the backdrop of forest and mountain, darker than the morning, he flapped his arms against the star-glittered sky and hugged himself. "Oh, but she cooks, our little woman does. She can plow the ground in any direction, she shoes horses, and milks herds of cows, and she plucks the chickens. Oh, what a splendid present she will be for Mama. Hurry up the horses; let's get her home before she freezes." As he recounted the list of my nonexistent talents, a squat silver moon rolled from under a cover of clouds and perched like a hen on his shoulder. I felt as though I had gotten off the train and had stepped out into an alien world. This was not the world I had asked for. Because it was still unfamiliar, there seemed to be not the slightest shred of beauty. My unaccustomed eyes saw nothing but a frozen world, bleak and harsh, without any hint of the glamour, the wealth, the romance I had so set my heart on finding. I had neither the patience nor the wisdom to realize that in time this world would become as familiar to me, and twice as dear, as what I had left behind. I am a person who fears change. The unknown is a threat until I learn its secrets. I am not proud of this, nor can I explain it; it's simply the way I am. Even the moon perched on Papa Joe's shoulder made me afraid.

"Gabriella?"

I tried to ignore him.

"Gabriella, little treasure, speak to me."

I was cold, so very cold. I tried to speak but could not. Papa Joe tented the quilt about me, making a place where I could be warm.

"Gabriella, are you well?"

"Yes." My voice was a rasp.

"You are shaking, little treasure, shaking like an aspen leaf."

"Ah-ha!" said Ambrose. "Just what we need, a sick dwarf. You always choose the runt of the litter, Papa Joe. This time's no different. I say toss her out, feed her to the coyotes. She's not even worth a train ticket back."

"Pay him no mind, little woman, my pet. He is worthless, let him go. Only don't die, promise you won't." Papa Joe sat on the bearskin beside me. He wrapped his long arms around me, singing and crooning as he held me to warm me, and I felt his strength and life flow into me, making me strong. "We're almost there," he said over and over, "almost there. We're going home."

Throughout the long ride, the team had been pulling up a long gentle incline, through forest and clearing. Now and then the iron rim of a wheel struck sparks from a rock, and Papa Joe said we should thank Mary and Joseph that the snow wasn't deep, or we never would make it at all. I had grown used to the strained breathing of the team, Butte and Bess, to the constant jingling of harness, to the muttered threats of Ambrose. The bucket of bricks had lost much of its warmth, and the wagon jolted sharply this way or that, rattling the bricks in their container.

Now the team bore sharply to the right, to start up a snowy mountain road, much steeper than before, and designed in a pattern of switchbacks to be easier on the horses. Shadows on the crusted surfaces of snow changed from a midnight blue to a softened blue-lilac; the horizon brightened, and the sun moved closer to daybreak. Silhouettes of pine and spruce stood stark against the lilac-shaded snow, and when at last the horses gained the top of the long steep hill, the road leveled onto a drifted plateau, and a vast valley, like a bowl of night, lay below us. Snow-capped mountains rimmed the far edge of the bowl, their rigid peaks catching fire as the sun shone upon them. I could never have imagined the West would look like this. It was like looking on God himself, not on His love, but on His power and glory. His love to me then seemed as distant as those icebound peaks burning in the early sun.

Papa Joe pointed out the sights. "What you see down there is the great Flathead Valley, and over there in the timber . . . see it? . . . like a drift of smoke, well, that isn't smoke, it's mist rising off the river. And over there . . ." he swung a mittened hand ". . . that is Kelly Hill, and that's where we'll go to pick huckleberries. Got to look out for bears, though. Bears are mean."

"Mean but not crazy," Ambrose said from the front. "You're stuffing her head full of nonsense. Another twenty-four hours with you and she'll be just as crazy."

Papa Joe gave me a wink. "Let him go. The boy is worse than any Swede. And that's all he can think about, how he wants to be a Swede. We've got too many Swedes out here as it is." He laughed aloud, showing all his white teeth in the dark of the morning. "Oh, but it was lucky for you the day you answered that ad. See down there, see the river? That's where we'll take you swimming in the summer, and fishing . . . do you like to fish? And that's where you can go skating. You can use Katie's skates, and oh, but you'll love it."

I loved it already. "Oh, yes," I said, caught up. "I see!

I saw myself speeding down the frozen river on my silver skates, Papa Joe in his hat and his greatcoat speeding along beside me.

Ambrose cracked his whip over the backs of the horses. "We send her back tomorrow."

Papa Joe set his jaw in a stubborn line. "We'll soon find out who's crazy, who's not."

As we drew nearer to the farmhouse, a black-and-white farm collie came rushing down the snowy lane to greet us. He jumped into the wagon, licked me in the face, and jumped out again, racing ahead to announce our arrival. His barking rang like a hammer against the iron air.

Fields and fields of drifted snow fringed with black pines, here and there dead cornstalks leaned into each other to prop each other up; Papa Joe knew what fears were in my mind, for he drew me close enough to whisper in my ear, "Just act nice, and they'll like you well enough."

The horses quickened their pace. Beyond a pencil line of broken fence, a herd of spotted cows stood at attention, and when we had passed them, they let out a chorus of bawling, trotting along the fence as far as the barnyard, their udders swinging awkwardly between their back legs. Their behavior did nothing to set me at ease. What if I had to catch them and milk them?

"There it is!" Papa Joe cried, "the house!"

"What did you expect?" Ambrose grumbled.

Above a shelterbelt of trees, a red brick chimney appeared with its silky feather of smoke, then an upstairs window blinking in the first shine of sun. The farm dog had worked himself into a frenzy with barking, and he galloped along beside us, only now and then breaking through the diamond-crust of snow.

Ambrose stopped the horses at the farmhouse

gate. Papa Joe swung himself lightly to the ground. He reached up his arms to swing me. "Come on, little woman. I will carry you in. Oh, but they are going to be pleased!"

I let him help me out, but I would not let him carry me in like a circus freak. He made an attempt to hoist me up to his shoulders, but I could be as stubborn as he. "I go in under my own steam," I said through clenched teeth. "Or I won't go in at all."

He looked as if I'd punched him.

"I mean what I say."

He shoved his fur hat back farther on his head, raised one shaggy black brow. "O-kay."

Ambrose crowed from his perch above the team. "You've met your match for mulishness, Papa Joe. Ten to one she'll own the farm at the end of one year."

I fitted my crutches under my arms and waited while Papa Joe lifted my suitcase and books from out of the wagon. Ambrose clucked the horses up, trotted them through the barnyard gate, and trotted them on toward the barn. The morning sun had risen above the far line of mountains and touched the house and the barn with its light, though it still gave no warmth.

Papa Joe led the way, through the gate, down the icy walk, up to the steps to the back porch. "This way, little woman. Don't fall on the ice, you might break something. Mind the steps. Here we go." He opened the screen door, opened the heavy wooden door and held it. Inside the porch he stomped his boots on a burlap bag thrown down for that purpose, and I stomped my school oxfords. He opened the next door, into the kitchen.

"Surprise!" he called out, as I hobbled in. "Surprise!"

# 8

So began my new life.

In spite of all my objections, Papa Joe swooped me up and stood me on a chair in the center of the kitchen. As I reeled with confusion and embarrassment, he shouted out, "Come around, everybody, see what I've brought. It's a present for Mama. That's why we went to the station." He threw back his head and laughed. "You thought we went to pick up some laying hens, but look, it wasn't hens we went for at all. So much better than hens. Mama! Where's Mama? Tell her to hurry. I've brought her a present."

Two blond children sat at a table, round-eyed at what they saw. A dark-haired young woman sat beside them, a cup lifted midway to her mouth. "What?" she asked, almost crossly. "What is it?"

*It?* This was what I'd come to?

"It's a chore girl," Papa Joe said happily. "Turn around, Gabriella, let them see you."

My balance on the chair was precarious at best. I ducked my head, took a tighter grip on my crutches, and glared.

A plump woman with ragged gray hair and a faded sweater came into the room. "Present?" she asked. "A present for me? What kind of present?"

"Birthday present," shouted Papa Joe.

"But it isn't my birthday." She studied me up and down.

"Christmas, then, it's a Christmas present."

"But it's too soon for a Christmas present."

"It's a *before* Christmas present. That's what it is, a *before* Christmas present." With a wink and a chuckle, a great boom of laughter, he flapped about the room, his dark eyes bright as two black coals.

"But what kind of present is it?" the woman insisted. "What does it do?"

"It's a chore girl."

"But I've never asked for a chore girl."

Papa Joe stopped his mad flight. "But you did ask for a chore girl, you did. You're always asking for a chore girl."

"I wanted a pot scrubber, that's what I asked for."

"Oh." He stared dumbly at the gray-headed woman, then he stared dumbly at me. "Oh."

"I can scrub pots," I said. "I can scrub fast or I can scrub slow. Any way you want them, I can scrub them."

The dark-haired girl at the table put her cup down. "It speaks."

"Of course she speaks," Papa Joe said. "This little woman is a treasure, and easy to keep. You will bless the day I brought her into the house."

"She's not going to live here?" Mama said.

"Of course she is going to live here, she's ours, ours forever."

"Oh, surely not," Mama said. She peered at me closely. "No."

"Yes," said Papa Joe, his face alight with pride of possession. "She's ours."

"I don't believe this," Mama said. "What have you gone and done now?"

The children sat at the table, silent as two stone cherubs, until the little boy said, "Is that all of it? It's awfully small."

"That's all there was at the station," said Papa Joe. Even he began to look doubtful, and I grew frightened that he really might try to send me back. "Maybe I'm small," I said, "but I'm powerful."

At this, the dark-haired girl began to giggle.

"Oh, my," said Mama Shevala. Her face darkened with doubt.

Papa Joe beamed. "She's a quick one, our little treasure. But she's tired and cold. Heat up the kettle, Tasha, make her some tea. I'll take her up and put her to bed in Katie's old room. Katie's not using it, not anymore."

He fixed me a place in a deep feather bed, and when the tea had come up on a tray, along with two homemade doughnuts and a slab of hot applesauce cake, he waited until I had warmed myself with the tea and had eaten every crumb of the cake and the doughnuts, before leaving me alone to undress myself and crawl under the big puffy comforters.

Already I was beginning to feel like a different person. I was determined to become a different person. I'd had quite enough of who I was. I'd still have to work around my physical imperfections, but I could do it; I knew I could. Whatever was asked of me I would cheerfully do. My good nature and my willing ways would win their hearts. I would make the She-vala family love me, all of them. Even Ambrose.

I fell into a deep sleep and slept well into the afternoon, waking to a pale winter light from the window. I sat up slowly, listened, and, hearing no movement downstairs, I threw back the covers and slipped to the floor.

"Gabriella?" It was Mama.

"Yes, ma'am."

"Gabriella, if you're up and about, do have a wash and come down for a bite to eat. Then we'll decide what's to be done with you." This was expressed in the gentlest of tones. It could have been spoken by doves.

I found a washbasin and pitcher of water on a straight-back chair in a corner of the room. The water was as cold as the room, but that didn't matter. I washed myself and used a thick white towel that someone had left folded over the chair back, to dry myself. I combed my hair, pulled on the faded brown dress, spoke briefly to Heaven, and started down the stairs—work to do, hearts to win.

Mama was at her sewing machine in the parlor. She looked different somehow, pumping away on the treadle machine. She had thrown a black woolen shawl across her shoulders and wore black woolen stockings on her plump little legs. A wisp of white hair had pulled loose from a comb, and she puffed at it as she ran a piece of flannel back and forth beneath the needle. A fire hissed and crackled in an iron heater.

"There you are," she said, not looking at me. "I've put the kettle on for tea, and I've just taken the kolachi out of the oven. I'll fix you one, you must be hungry."

89

I followed her into the kitchen.

"Now," she said, "Gabriella, I've set water on to boil so that you can commence with your morning chores—though it *is* afternoon. I don't know what your situation was there in the city, but here in the country you may find us somewhat primitive. We get our water from a pump in the yard, and we keep our fires going with wood we chop ourselves. When the woodbox is empty, you must run out to the woodshed for more. We must never, *never* let the fires go out. Once the house is cold, it is very hard to ever get it warm again." She focused on a point about a foot above my head. "You do understand, don't you?"

"Completely. I understand completely."

"You will need an apron, dear. Have you any?"

I had not.

"If you stay to work for us you will need an apron. *If*, I say. Nothing's settled."

She fixed me a place at the big kitchen table. "Tea and kolachi? Will that be enough?"

"That will be lovely."

"Cream?"

"Thank you."

She poured the tea, selected a fragrant sweet roll from the dozen or so cooling on racks in the center of the table, and then excused herself to return to her sewing, leaving me alone with all the kolachi. Never had I tasted anything so delicious. It was manna from heaven, it was everything I'd ever wanted, it was excitement and adventure: it was my new life. As large as my two fists put together, each warm golden kolachi was dusted seductively with just a touch of flour and had a hollow at the center filled with a sweetish paste of poppy seeds ground with walnuts and mixed with honey. I made short work of the first kolachi, washed it down with milky tea, then gobbled up a second. The third went down as pleasantly as those that went before. I was reaching for another when Mama came in to explain the work I was to do.

"You like the kolachi?" she asked, eyeing what remained on the racks.

"It is delicious." I wiped the crumbs off my face.

"The recipe comes all the way from Bohemia, by way of southern Russia—passing through Kimball, Nebraska, to get here."

"What a nice long way to come." I wished she'd go back to her sewing, so I could have one more—just one would be enough. Kolachi was all I could think of. I found myself staring at them. My head buzzed. "You must be very busy . . ." I'd grown brassy with desire. ". . . Don't let me keep you from your sewing."

"First I must explain the cream separator, how to wash it. I'll take it apart and show you how it's done, but it is very important that you clean it thoroughly, and you must put it together exactly as I show you before the men come in from their four o'clock milking." As she spoke she crossed the kitchen and opened the door to the milk porch, never once looking me in the eye. I could have been a kitchen chair, a teapot, a doorknob, for all the recognition she gave me. She came back into the kitchen with a large steel bowl in her arms. She set the bowl down on the counter by the sink and, staring into the middle distance, puffed at the wisp of runaway hair. "Have you ever worked on a farm, Gabriella?"

"I'm quick to learn."

The shadow of a frown flitted across her face.

"Tell me anything, tell me once, I'll remember it always. I'll go to my grave and never forget."

The corners of her mouth turned down.

"We shall see," she said.

I'm ashamed to admit that I didn't grasp a single word of the explanation. I didn't realize that the men would come in with buckets of milk, still hot from the cows, to pour into the steel bowl at the top of the separator, that they would turn the crank on the side of the machine until the milk began to filter from the bowl, through the graduated disks inside the separator, and that it would pour from the spouts— skimmed milk into one waiting bucket, cream into a cream can. My mind did not focus on any of these details. My mind was sitting at the table gorging itself on kolachi.

"Now then, Gabriella . . ." Mama Shevala glanced around. "I'll fetch you a stepstool so you can stand at the sink. No, that's not high enough, is it? We'll pull this chair up, and . . . no, still not right. Here, try this catalog, stand on that . . . there, that's better. No? Better without the catalog? Now then, what shall we do with your crutches? Are you all right up there without them? Yes?" She leaned the troublesome crutches against the base of the counter, and they clattered to the floor. "Oh . . . this will simply *have* to do." In a burst of irritation, she kicked them out of her way.

"First, hot water . . ." She carried a bucket of steaming water from the stove, poured the water into the dishpan, added soap, got me a dishrag, got me a bottle brush, sighed. Then she set all the disengaged separator parts out on the counter and put the large steel bowl into the dishpan. She got a second bucket of water from the stove, poured it into another dishpan in the sink for rinse water. With a long sad sigh, she returned to the parlor to work on her sewing.

At last. Alone with the cooling kolachi.

I climbed down from my chair and ate two of them standing at the table. Then to work: I scrubbed at the steel bowl with the soapy rag, brushed the inside of the spouts with the bottle brush, took the pyramid of graduated disks apart . . . and nearly fainted. The smell of sour milk was almost more than I could stand. I took a deep breath and scrubbed with vigor. Water ran down my arms and dripped from elbows—I'd mop up later, when I'd built up my strength with another kolachi.

Two kolachis later, I waded through the water that had spilled on the floor, climbed back onto my chair, and renewed my vigor. I clenched my jaws against the terrible smell, determined to clean the separator better than it had ever been cleaned before. The Shevalas would bless the day Papa Joe found me. Oh, but they would love me!

A chill in the air brought me out of my dream; I'd forgotten the stove. I found a short-handled poker and lifted the lid from the firebox. A few orange coals glowed on the grate. I took sticks of kindling from the woodbox, thrust them into the stove, prayed they would catch . . . but they didn't. I blew on the coals, which only raised a fine ash, and I tried again, puffing out my cheeks like a goddess of wind, but not a lick of flame. The kitchen grew colder.

"*Yoo hoo?*" It was Mama Shevala, calling from the parlor.

"*Yoo hoo?*" I yodeled back.

"*Yoo hoo?* Gabriella?"

"*Com-ing,*" I sang.

I wadded up a piece of butcher's paper from the bottom of the woodbox, and I pushed the wad down among the dying coals. When it flared and died, I pushed in another stick of kindling. Nothing but smoke. I grabbed up a bleached white tea towel hanging from a rack beside the stove and shook it at the smoke, to shoo it out of the kitchen, but it didn't shoo. Meanwhile, the kitchen got colder and colder.

*"Yoo hoo?"*

I dropped the tea towel, grabbed my crutches, and hurried to the parlor.

Mama looked up and eyed my soaking dress. "How's it going in the kitchen, Gabriella?"

"It's going very well."

"I see."

The sins of the kitchen had not caught up with the parlor. A fire crackled merrily in the little pot-bellied stove beside Mama's sewing machine, drawing Mama and her baskets of mending, her flannels and pattern papers, her rickracks and laces, her flour-sack calicoes, into its spell of warmth and well-being. Portraits of ancestors looked down on the scene with approval: bearded men in stiff collars, women in fanciful hairdos, children in their christening suits; they looked as if they had been there forever, watching. Someday my portrait would join them. Generations of Shevalas would someday sing my praises. *We couldn't have gotten on without her,* they'd say. *What a saint, that Gabriella!*

Mama's thoughts were on aprons.

She snipped the last thread and held out her creation. "Such a nice pattern, don't you think? I've been saving this pattern for something special."

The tiniest hearts and flowers waltzed across the skirt and the bib. There were two heart-shaped pockets edged with rickrack and frothy with lace, which put me in mind of Rowena LeSage.

"Well? Do you like it?"

94

"It's like you opened me up and looked inside at all my thoughts and feelings."

"You do say odd things, Gabriella."

It was then I felt the chill creeping in from the kitchen. It was then I thought of the train in the station waiting to carry me back to St. Louis.

"Let me check that hem," Mama said. She reached into her pocket and whipped out her tape and her pins.

"It's fine, just fine."

"Climb upon this chair, Gabriella. There's nothing I hate worse than a draggy hem." She pulled the apron on, down over my head, and tied it in back. Just a hint of smoke make my nose twitch, but Mama didn't notice it. "Turn around," she said, "this will take but a minute."

"Oh, it's perfect . . . perfect. I love it just the way it is. I'll treasure it always, wear it night and day. I'll hand it on to my children and my children's children . . ."

"It's yours for as long as you stay, Gabriella. I can't promise more." She pinned the hem to her liking, then pulled it off, up over my head, nearly taking my nose in the process. "You'd best get on with your work," she said. "The men will be in with the milk, and they're going to need the separator."

I climbed down, feeling woozy, woozy from kolachi or woozy from fear—I didn't know which—my legs so weak they could have been jointed to bend either way. I felt like a rag doll, grabbing up my crutches and hobbling back into the kitchen, as Mama called after me, "I'll be in in a minute, Gabriella, to see how you are doing."

My heart leaped up and froze midair.

The scene in the kitchen had grown worse in my

absence: dark smoke boiled up out of the cookstove; the wood I'd pushed into the firebox had done nothing but smolder, and the room was freezing. Water in the dishpan had turned to scum, like my life. There was nothing to do but to buck up my spirits by eating the rest of the kolachi, which I did. And then I turned to the separator, fitting parts together any way I could get them to fit. I carried the whole thing out to the stand on the milk porch, settled the bowl on the top, the spouts below the big bowl, and then . . . there was a piece left over, a small black rubber ring, just the right size and color for a halo gone bad. I shoved it behind some gallon honey jars that were sitting on the window ledge, just as the men came up the walk from the barn. I heard their boots clunking up the steps and I fled back into the kitchen.

"*Yoo hoo?*"

I yoo-hooed back, without enthusiasm. My life was over. I knew what was going to happen. Mama came into the kitchen, a vague figure behind the roiling smoke. She moved toward me, her arms out like a sleepwalker walking through the dark, feeling her way so she wouldn't bump into the table or chairs, but then she stepped in a puddle of water and her feet went up as she went down, and she gave a little scream as she fell.

Out on the milk porch, the men were pouring the milk from their buckets into the bowl on the separator stand, making a noisy rush and a slosh as the milk went in, and then one began turning the handle, and the milk spilled to the floor with such a roar and a crash it could have been Niagara.

"What . . .?" shouted Papa Joe.

"It's *her!*" Ambrose shouted. "*Her!* The dwarf!"

In the kitchen Mama gave a long sad wail.

"Ruined!" she cried. "Everything's ruined. What did I do to deserve this?"

I didn't wait to hear any more. I thrust my crutches snug beneath my arms and left the kitchen as fast as I could, up the stairs to the bedroom, where I slammed the door and hid myself under the bed.

# 9

They would have shipped me back the next morning, except that Mama Shevala came up to my room shortly after I'd disgraced myself and found me feverish and still beneath the big bed. Papa Joe saddled old Thunder to ride through the snow all the way to the Halvorson farm where he could telephone the doctor. Hours later the doctor arrived, driving up to the house in his noisy Ford, running into the house, and hurrying up to my room.

"It's a good thing you called when you did," I heard him tell the Shevalas. "If you'd waited much longer we might have lost her."

I observed this scene through a haze of pain: the older Shevalas standing over me, humble and apologetic, while the doctor rapped my chest, thumped my back, and listened to my heart with his cold silver stethoscope. "By rights," he said, "she ought to be in the hospital, sick as she is. But I wouldn't want to move her. She's delicate, very frail." He put his face close to mine and shone a bright light into my eyes. "It's possible she may never be well again."

I knew he was wrong, that he *had* to be wrong! I wanted to jump up from the bed and tell him so. There were so many more things I had yet to do. I wanted to climb Kelly Hill, as Papa Joe promised. I wanted to skate down a frozen river, my head bent into the thrill of my speed, arms pumping, silver skates flashing. I wanted to taste summer in the country. I wanted long walks down country lanes, and I wanted to find my brown-eyed young man . . . I had to find him, to see him once more, I *had* to. "I will get better," I insisted, speaking through the dizziness and the sickness that held me. I tried to prop myself up on one elbow, but the doctor gently put me down again. "Not now," he said. "You must lie still, get plenty of rest, take your medicine . . . if you're going to get well."

"*See?*" Ambrose crowed from the doorway. "What did I tell you? She'll send us to the poorhouse yet."

Papa Joe crossed the room in two angry strides. He grabbed Ambrose by the arm and shoved him out into the hall. "Where is your heart?" Papa Joe shouted, and Ambrose yelled back, "It's your head that's confused, you old fool!"

There was the sound of a weight striking the floor, sliding down the steps, and then Papa Joe returned to my side, his face looking dark and strong, his black hair disheveled. "Don't you worry, little treasure," he said, peering down at me. "We'll see that you get well. You shall have the best of everything. Nothing is too good for our speckled hen. Don't worry about Ambrose, he's a nincompoop, a nothing."

"And you're not helping her any yourself," the doctor said. "I want the lot of you out of her room. How can I get on with my treatment when the two of you are lummoxing around?"

Enough has been written about sickness; I won't inflict those memories. Penicillin had yet to be accepted by all doctors. My doctor didn't want to prescribe it out of fear of dangerous reactions. He did give me a bottle of bitter liquid to ease my pain and to help me sleep. "If you notice a change, if you think you're getting worse, have Papa Joe climb back onto that old nag of his and get down to the Halvorsons' farm where he can use the phone. There's been bad blood between Shevalas and Halvorsons, but Papa Joe sets great store by you, Gabriella. He'd do anything for you." The doctor placed a cool hand on my brow. "You are a person of very strong will. I don't want you to worry, you'll pull through."

For days on end I lay close to death. Through the long days and nights Papa Joe stayed by my side, leaving only now and then to go outside for chores. Even if I was sleeping when he returned to the room, the cold he brought with him, and the strong smell of horses, cows, and hay, told me he was there and knowing this made me feel better.

Sometimes I found him bending over me, his eyes like black coals, the straight black hair swung down across his eyes. Was I hungry? he wanted to know. Was I cold? Wouldn't I *please* try another sip of tea? Pudding? Soup? Bread with jam? He gave me his pocketwatch to listen to. He brought me a big bouquet of weeds, dried weeds, stuck in a mayonnaise jar. He brought me a bouquet of feathers: rooster feathers, pheasant feathers, spotted peafowl feathers; he brought me the tail feathers of a peacock he'd seen once on a trip. He promised he would buy me a peacock, a pair, if only I'd get well. He promised me a pony and cart. He promised he'd dress me up in spangled tights and show me at the county fair. He'd find me a little dwarf man, so I wouldn't be lonesome. "You can be the king and queen of Dwarfland," he promised, if only I'd get up from my bed.

I hated him.

While Papa Joe was at his morning chores in the barnyard, Mama came in with a basin of water so I could bathe myself. Businesslike, thorough, she said she'd always wanted to be a nurse when she was growing up, but that she'd gotten carried away in the romance department and had married Papa Joe instead. She said I wasn't to feel bad about staying in bed, that getting sick could happen to anyone. And as far as the spilled milk was concerned, that could have happened to anyone, too. She seemed to be more at ease with me when I was down in bed than when I'd been up and hobbling around. She made me three pretty nightgowns and a bed jacket, each trimmed in white eyelet threaded with blue satin ribbon.

One morning after my bath Papa Joe came in with a kitten and put it down on my pillow. At that time I still felt too weak and too ill to face a creature as unfamiliar to me as the homely little kitten. When I shut my eyes against it, it stuck its cold nose against my cheek and mewed a plaintive note that sounded like *me? me?* My eyes jumped open, and I heard Papa Joe chuckle. "Even the cat loves you now, Gabriella. If you die, you'll break its heart."

It wasn't a cute kitten; its eyes were mere slits that squinted at the light, and as small as it was its ears were outrageously large. It was a dull gray rat color, and it sprawled across the pillowcase Mama had just that morning put on my pillow. It yowled until Papa Joe took it away.

Next morning it was there again, yowling, squinting at the light, seeking about with its oversized head, brushing my face with its whiskers. When I shut my eyes against it, Papa Joe scolded me. "Cats are heaven's ambassadors, you know. They were placed here on earth to test us. Jesus said as much himself: 'Whatever you do to the least of these, you do also to me.' Now, some might say that Jesus was talking about kids, but I say *cats*. Kittens are born in stables, just like our Lord. And they're born around Christmastime, and what could be so meek and so mild as a kitten?"

He rubbed the kitten's ears with a callused thumb. The kitten leaped up, grabbed Papa Joe's thumb, and bit it. Papa Joe yelped. He looked so surprised I had to laugh. It was the first time I'd laughed in a very long time.

Papa Joe's black brows shot up. He jumped to his feet and, in his long-legged, loose-jointed stride, hurried to the head of the stairs. "Hey! Everybody! She's better, Gabriella is better!"

There was a moment of silence, then Mama called back, "Ask if she'd like a nice pudding."

"I would," I said, reaching out to rub the kitten's gray head.

Papa Joe tore down the stairs and came back with the pudding himself.

As the days crept closer to Christmas, I was able to sit up and sip hot sugared tea and nibble graham crackers. Tasha, the haughty sixteen-year-old daughter, came and went with bowls of hot soup, boiled chicken with dumplings, fresh-baked bread with churned butter, rich puddings full of raisins. The most exotic of all the Shevalas, she moved with a gypsy grace, up and down the stairs, never speaking to me, acting as though I were less important than the shadows that followed her evening lantern. I admired her. Tall and slim, with long black hair, ivory skin, slanted obsidian eyes, she seemed more romantic than Rowena LeSage.

Throughout this time, the doctor paid several visits to the farm to check on my progress. "You've got the constitution of an ox," he told me at the end of one visit. "There's nothing in my medical bag that can do half as much as a strong constitution. With it you can survive almost any disaster, without it you perish." Then he looked me in the eye. "Now, tell me what's going on in your mind? You're looking very thoughtful, Gabriella."

Until he asked, I had not been aware of my feelings of loneliness, but now the tears began to run down my face, and I wiped at them with my hands. "It's just that . . . just that I never have anyone, anyone to talk to . . ."

"The Shevalas are kind?" He peered at me closely through his steel-rimmed glasses. Puffs of white hair behind each ear gave him an owlish expression.

"They are very kind. But . . . I . . . I feel out of place here." The tears streamed down my face so that it took me a moment or so before I could go on. "I'm always afraid they'll send me away . . . I've done everything wrong. They'll try to send me back to Missouri, and nobody back there . . ." My voice dropped to a whisper because I felt so ashamed of what I had to confess. ". . . nobody there wants me, either. My aunt will put me into an . . . institution."

"I see." Gently, with the edge of a blanket, he wiped the tears from my face. "You could do with some cheering up. What you need is some company."

"I have plenty of *company*."

"I mean *real* company, a visitor, and I think I've got just the right person, a young friend of mine . . ."

"Oh, I don't know . . ." I didn't want anyone to see me as I was just then. "I still feel weak."

"It could be what you need to get you on your feet again."

I had almost forgotten this conversation, when one afternoon, as I was sitting among my pillows, too tired to read, still too weak to get out of bed, too bored to sleep. I heard a knock at the door, then: "*Yoo hoo?*"

"Come in," I called back, not really caring. I had been entertaining myself by watching a square of sunlight move across the linoleum of my floor as the sun moved across my frosted window.

"Yoo hoo? Gabriella? Are you decent?"

I thought this over. "No."

I heard a nervous little laugh, then Mama Shevala said, "I've brought someone to see you. May we come in?"

I snatched my lacy bedjacket from the bottom of the bed, grabbed up a comb, gave my tangled hair twenty licks, and spit on my thumb to smooth my eyebrows into an arch as I'd seen the lovely Tasha do. "Okay."

Mama came into the room, her cheeks pink, her eyes shining. "The doctor has sent you a visitor, dear—a nice young man." She pushed a wisp of hair back behind one tortoise-shell comb. "He's a minister, Gabriella, so be on your best behavior." She whispered this last, then ushered him in. "Gabriella, Reverend Brentwood."

And there he was, just as I'd always dreamed, my brown-eyed young man. He put out one hand . . . touched my hand. He spoke. "Hello."

"Hello." I felt hot and cold all at the same time. My face felt like Jell-O for all its quivering, and I was amazed to hear myself speak, for all the shock and joy that stunned me.

"We meet again," he said.

"We meet again."

Mama looked puzzled. "You know each other?"

"Yes," I said.

At the very same moment, he said, "No."

I felt as if I'd been caught in a lie, and I stammered out an explanation: "We . . . we don't really know each other . . . that is, not really . . . not yet, but . . ." I looked to him for help.

"We met on the train," he said smoothly, coolly, and with infinite charm. "I was returning from a conference, and Gabriella was on her way to Montana. We both changed trains in Chicago."

"On a train?" Mama said, her cheeks growing pinker. "Can you fancy that? Meeting on a train? Now, what a nice coincidence. I must leave you two alone to get to know each other better. If you need anything, give a holler."

When she'd gone, my brown-eyed young man pulled up a chair and sat down beside my bed. I was glad I'd taken the time to brush my hair. I hoped against hope that he'd notice the ribbons and lace on the bedjacket that Mama had made for me. I hoped he'd notice the flutter of my heart so that his would flutter, too. I hoped most of all that he would see me, the real *me*, the person inside, who loved him.

"You're looking well," he said, "considering."

"You look well, too."

He was dressed in white shirt, blue suit, blue tie, gold cuff links each with a tiny diamond chip, shoes polished so perfectly they shone like dark mirrors. I committed him to memory, every detail.

He smiled. "I thought I'd lost track of you forever."

"Oh," I said, heartfelt, "so did I."

"I guess the Lord had other plans."

"Sometimes He's like that."

Timothy smiled. "Sometimes He is."

And so we proceeded.

I can't say exactly what we talked about on that cold winter's day upstairs in my room, or even if we talked at all; if there were words, these words were only tokens of what we could not speak aloud. The looks that passed between us were drawn from the heart's own silence. Two trains speeding in opposite directions freeze in place. When I looked into those warm brown eyes and found him looking back, when he smiled on me, when he listened to the stories I told about my life (stories I had never told anyone), when he listened to me, accepted me, I basked in his presence like a lizard in the sun.

Before he left he talked about his calling. He talked about salvation. He talked about the Lord and how He loved us. We had a little prayer, then had another. He gave me his blessing, and I took it. "I'd like to visit you again," he said. "If you don't mind."

"I'd like that very much."

And then he kissed me, on the forehead, and when I opened my eyes from this miracle, he had gone and had left me floating in an ocean of euphoria. I felt as if he'd gathered up all the weariness, worry, and discouragement that I had known throughout my life and had left me stronger, more hopeful.

That same evening, Papa Joe came in for his usual before-meal visit and found me out of bed, dressed in my everyday clothes, ready to go downstairs to eat supper with the family. Even with Timothy's kiss still burning on my brow, it took all the courage I could muster to leave my safe, but cold, little room and to face my new life once again.

# 10

My first experience with the family at the table proved to be less frightening than I had imagined. Ambrose had gone hunting for deer in the forest along the river and had not yet returned, the children had gone to a birthday party on a neighboring farm, and Tasha was "out."

"Out where?" Papa Joe asked.

"She didn't say," Mama said. "And I didn't ask. I'm so worried about that Ambrose I can't think straight. Who knows what goes on in those woods this time of night?"

We were eating boiled chicken in gravy with mashed potatoes, and I was having some trouble holding a chicken leg to the plate with my fork while hacking it up with my knife. Papa Joe had tied a big napkin around his neck and let the gravy fall where it would. "With that mouth of his, Ambrose's safer out in the woods than here," Papa Joe said.

Mama glared at him. "I was thinking about the Halvorson boys. Hard telling what kind of trouble they could get into, with all of them armed with hunting rifles, and after what happened out at the grange."

Papa Joe bent over his plate. "If he plays with fire, he's going to get burned. One of these days they're going to catch him good and work him over."

"You're the meanest man I've ever known, Papa Joe." Mama got up from the table and started stacking dirty dishes. "You've got no feeling for flesh and blood. It's not natural the way you are."

Papa Joe turned to me and winked.

I winked back, and this tickled him so that he launched into a lively Bohemian tune that involved a great deal of foot stomping, knee slapping, and silverware banging. I had never seen anyone act so strangely and hardly knew how to behave, for I didn't want to encourage him, nor did I want to offend him. His wild behavior matched the feelings that Timothy's visit had started up in me, and I had no more idea of how to handle those feelings than I knew how to act when Papa Joe flew into one of his fits. Nothing in my life had prepared me for either.

Shortly after supper I went back up to my room to go to bed. With all that had happened that day I had become very tired but was so keyed up it took forever for me to fall asleep. In the meantime I heard the children come in, then Ambrose and his angry yelps. "Tasha?" I heard him shout. And then: "*Halvorson's* . . . that's where she's gone! She's seeing that no good Nils Halvorson! I'll wring her neck when she gets home!"

As the hours went by, the house turned dark and still, and as I drifted off to sleep I thought of Tasha in the arms of her forbidden lover, how she was like me, how one day I would rest in the arms of my brown-eyed young man—Timothy. In my own selfish way I was glad that Ambrose had turned his wrath on his sister. Now that I was better and would be going downstairs, I didn't want Ambrose to turn all his hatred on me. My every breath became a prayer that the Shevalas wouldn't send me away.

Early next morning Tasha entered my room to bring my morning tea with two hot kolachi. I had planned to be up and dressed so I could eat downstairs with the family, but I'd overslept and was still in my bed. Before I had a chance to explain, she had put the tray down on the bedside table, and, with a rattle of beads and a swish of her skirts, she was gone.

I had thrown back the comforters to slip out of bed, when Papa Joe knocked at my door and called, "Gabriella? Little treasure? I have a surprise for you."

"What kind of surprise?"

"Visitors."

I jerked the comforter back up to my neck. I thought at once of Timothy, but it couldn't be him, not at this hour. Papa Joe's idea of visitors could be anything from a pair of hairy barn spiders to a box of baby mice. On that particular morning I wasn't in the mood for spiders or mice. "Wait!" I called out. "I'm not decent."

"Then get decent, quick! I've got some people out here who've been wanting to see you. They've been waiting and waiting, and they say they can't wait any longer."

I cast around for my hairbrush. I looked a fright, I knew it. "Who are they?"

"They're little like you, and they can't wait to see you."

*Little like me? Had Papa Joe remembered his promise to find me a little dwarf man?* I felt sick. I saw myself in spangled tights on exhibit at the county fair, and if my window had not been frozen shut I might have climbed out of it and galloped away across the crusted snow. I had no interest at all in meeting other freaks. I had found my true love, and my own true love had found me.

Beyond the door a small voice cried out: "Papa Joe, please, we want to see her. You promised. You said when she was well enough that we could go in and see her. We want to see the little dwarf woman."

"Don't say *dwarf*," a second voice said. "You'll hurt her feelings."

All the strength drained out of my body. The voices belonged to the children I'd seen the day of my arrival. I had been aware of them, had heard them playing, had worried that they might come into my room and find me, but until now I hadn't had to face them. My heart banged away like a drum; I was terrified of children. In my experience they were amoral, cruel, and as unpredictable as fate. In public places their mothers always tried to keep them from coming near me, not for *my* comfort, I'm afraid, but out of fear that my misfortune might rub off on the children.

"I'm sorry," I called to Papa Joe, "but I don't like children."

"Oh, but these are good children, little woman. You are going to love these children—I guarantee."

He threw open the door, and they came tumbling in like puppies. Eager, yet shy, they came up to the bed, then waited uneasily for some signal from me. At first they looked exactly alike—straight blond hair, light blue eyes, freckled noses. I waited for the usual reaction, but they stood their ground.

"I'm Katherine," the little girl said. She put out her hand. "You can call me Katie."

"I'm Charles." The little boy gave me a gap-toothed grin. "But don't call me Chuck, and *please* don't call me Chuckie."

I promised I would not.

"I like her already," he said to Papa Joe.

Papa Joe beamed.

Though I watched them closely, the children showed no signs of wanting to run away screaming, and in spite of myself I became quite interested in them and invited them to climb upon the bed, where they'd be more comfortable. Papa Joe settled himself in a straight-back chair, looking very pleased. He had brought the little gray goblin cat in the bib of his overalls. He took the cat out and it leaped from his arms to the bed, where it went into a wild display of acrobatics, chasing an imaginary mouse all around the children and beneath the rumpled comforter.

Katie and Charles squealed as he pounced on their feet.

"He's wonderful," Charles said.

Katie wanted to know his name.

I looked to Papa Joe. It hadn't occurred to me that the cat should have a name.

"It's Gabriella's cat," Papa Joe said. "She's the one who has to name him."

"His name's Goblin," I said, not thinking. "He's little and naughty, just like a goblin."

"Just like you," said Charles.

At this Katie flew at him. "That's mean, Charles. Don't say such mean things . . . Gabriella's not naughty."

Charles gave me a sly wicked look. "She is, too,

naughty. She messed up the separator and made Ambrose spill all the milk, and I don't care if she did, because Ambrose is the one who's mean. He deserved it."

At this Papa Joe slapped his knee and hooted. "Out of the mouths of children, oh, isn't it the truth? I knew you were going to like each other. What a marvelous thing that we sent for Gabriella."

And suddenly both children were hugging me, telling me how glad they were that I'd come to live at the farm, how lucky they were, how happy they were just to know me. I found myself with tears in my eyes. Luckily, Goblin chose just that moment to leap to the top of my head, where he sank his claws into my thick mass of hair and swung, like Tarzan from jungle vines, emitting his raucous *mr-r-r-rouw!* I let out a shriek and grabbed for him, but by then he had dropped to the bed and had sprung for Papa Joe's shoulder, where he began a mock attack on Papa Joe's ear and had us all laughing.

Later, when my visitors had gone, I dressed myself quickly, addressed myself to heaven—a few words of gratitude could not go amiss—tucked my crutches under my arms, and made my way down the stairs, prepared to fulfill my job as chore girl. The children's hugs and kisses still fresh around my neck, and with Timothy's attention to give me courage, I made my way through the parlor, through the dining room, and on toward the kitchen where I heard low tones of conversation.

"Oh, I don't know," Mama's voice was saying. "Ambrose may be right, she's more hindrance than help."

"But we want to keep her," Katie exclaimed.

"If you don't keep her," I heard Charles threaten, "I'll never eat my vegetables, and then you'll be sorry.

And I'll run away, and I'll never come back, and I'll take Gabriella with me. See if I don't."

*Oh.* I stood shocked and still. The Shevalas were deciding my fate.

"She is kind of cute," Tasha said.

"And she's good luck," said Papa Joe. "There's nothing as lucky as a little dwarf woman at work in the kitchen. It is old Bohemian wisdom."

"Stuff and nonsense," Mama said.

"So much for old Bohemian wisdom," Ambrose sneered. "Just look how far it has got us . . . nowhere."

"As long as I'm head of this family, she stays."

There was the sound of an argument, a brief scuffle, and Mama shrieked, "Enough of your rough stuff, both of you. You're going to break my *dishes.*"

I could not stand where I was forever, hoping, praying, quaking in my oxfords. By the time I'd made my way into the kitchen, only Mama and the children were there. Tasha was out on the milk porch rattling the big gallon milk cans, and the men had gone out to do chores.

Katie and Charles stared at me round-eyed, for the briefest of moments, then ran to throw their arms around me. "If they send you away, we're going, too," Charles cried. "We'll run away, and they'll never find us." Standing beside me, the six-year-old was only an inch or so shorter than I. Katie was several inches taller. Still, they loved me enough to defend me, and even though my whole future was at stake, I felt honored, treasured.

"Is it true?" I asked Mama Shevala. "Are you going to send me away? I ought to know. You have to tell me."

Mama had been kneading bread dough; flour covered her arms and dusted a smudge on her chin. She turned around to look at me, but glanced away before my eyes met hers. "My," she said, "where are your manners? Didn't anyone ever tell you not to listen in on other people's conversations? I thought people from the city were so persnickety. I thought it was only people from the country who were bumpkins."

"Mama," Katie said stoutly, "Gabriella wants to know, she *needs* to know if she can stay here or not. She has to make plans. It's so terrible never to know where you are going to live."

Mama plunged her arms back into the dough. "If Papa Joe says she can stay, she can stay. Unless, of course, she disgraces herself. And then, I'm afraid she must go."

"She won't disgrace herself," Charles said.

Katie agreed. "Besides, Papa Joe said Gabriella would bring us good luck, and I feel luckier already. We got a letter from our mother two days ago, and I got a good mark on my spelling test yesterday, and maybe if Gabriella stays, maybe I'll even pass arithmetic. But that would take a miracle."

"Katie's real dumb in arithmetic," Charles said.

"I'll help you with it, if you want me to."

"Do what you want," Mama said, punching down the dough with her fists, "but don't ever mess around in my kitchen again."

"I've always been good at arithmetic," I said. "I'd be glad to tutor the children."

"Good at arithmetic?" Mama said. "Who would have thought it?"

"I would have thought it," Charles said. He screwed his face up in a scowl. "Just because she's little, that doesn't mean she doesn't have brains."

I could have kissed him. "We'll get started right away."

An hour later, when the men came in from outside, the children and I were hard at work in front of the stove in the parlor. Katie was struggling with multiplication, Charles pored over his first grade reader, and I had dug through my box of books for *Beautiful Joe,* hoping I might interest the children in my favorite story.

With a snide remark, Ambrose went up to his room, but Papa Joe wanted to stay, to listen to the lessons and the reading. "Who would have thought?" he asked, after hearing the first sad story of that most wonderful of books. "Who would have thought that anyone would be smart enough to understand the language of dogs and to write that story down?"

Snow was falling outside the window, piling up on post and pine, drifting across the yard, closing us all in together. The fragrance of Mama's baking bread made the indoors as cozy and warm as the outdoors was cold and alien. I had been spared. I could stay. I would get to see *him* again.

"At least until the children's mother comes for them," Mama said.

"Who knows when that will be?" said Papa Joe.

"Oh, she'll be here, sooner or later," Mama said, complacently. "She said so in her letter. She said she'd be along as soon as she could get away—sometime before or after Christmas."

Papa Joe gave me a long-faced look. He had been working at a block of wood with his pocketknife. "Poor little thing," he said, his knife blade glinting in the firelight, "how could we send her away?"

I could not fall asleep that night, for thinking about life in an institution. Even there I would be forced to work hard to pay for board and room; Tante Eloise had painted this picture. I would scrub floors, peel potatoes all day long, mop up after the incontinent. I would never see *him* again, never be loved, except maybe by madmen. I felt the dark press down upon me and could not close my eyes. Moonlight made my frosted window glow. I slid out from under the comforters to go to the window and look out. I scratched a space in the frost flowers and peered through it as if to see my own future.

The snow had stopped falling; moonlight shone full upon the hummocks and drifts beyond the trees of the yard. I was thinking of Timothy, wondering if he might be thinking of me, when I noticed a shadowy figure moving across the wind-drifted snow. It was two figures, a man on horseback, and coming closer, approaching the house. For only a moment I thought it was *him*. But no. He glanced up at my window, glanced away, waited beneath the dark swaying pines, and then a second figure joined him, running across the yard, through the gate, and when he'd swung down from his horse, she was in his arms, her dark hooded shadow merging with his. It was Tasha. Tasha, but it could have been me. Someday it would be me. Even then, I knew this belief made me strong.

# 11

The children's mother was the oldest daughter of Mama and Papa Joe. Sometimes I used to wonder about her, whether she would be soft and gentle like Mama, or wildly eccentric like Papa Joe. I only hoped that she would never come back to the farm to claim the two children. Then, the day before Christmas, she wrote a letter, explaining that no matter how much she yearned to be with them at this most sacred of seasons, her work prevented it.

". . . I *ache* to be with you, dearest Katie and little Chuck, to hold you in my arms once again, but alas!! I cannot . . ." It was enough to make a person want to throw up. She said she'd come *after* Christmas, that she would take them back to Spokane, that she would smother them with hugs and kisses.

The children reacted with joy, while I boiled with resentment.

As the morning progressed, the household fell into an uproar. Wild with excitement, the children raced up and down the stairs with Shep the old farm collie, who had been let in as a special holiday treat. Normally, he slept out in the barn to guard the stanchioned milk cows, but now he was running at the heels of Katie and Charles, barking and barking. Mama stood at the kitchen worktable, up to her elbows in sweet dough, complaining that she had far too much to do, that she couldn't get it all done before Christmas.

"May I help?" I asked, still brooding.

"To tell the honest truth, Gabriella, you are not very helpful."

"But I want to help. That's why I'm here." I hurried to get my personal apron, then stood at the ready. "What needs to be done?"

She pushed her hair back with one thumb. "Oh, my. There's floors to mop, and more baking, and sewing. I want to finish the lace on Katie's new underslip so she'll have it to wear with her dress on Christmas. If this weather lets up we might even make it to mass Christmas Day."

"I can do the lace."

Their talk about sending me back made me daring. "Let me do the lace. I'm a genius at sewing."

With a mild blue eye she measured me up and down. "Gabriella, you have never used a needle."

"Oh, but I have."

She narrowed her frown. "You're sure, now?"

"Just call me Miss Muffet."

She turned this around in her mind. "It *would* be a help."

"I always did sewing back in Missouri. People

119

there are very particular about their sewing, and they all claimed that I was the best." When I said this I knew it was a lie, but as I went on it almost seemed to be true. "My specialty was lace," I said, "sewing it on."

Mama let go of a sigh. "It would give me time to finish the baking, and I could finish the shirts I'm making for Ambrose and Papa Joe, if you won't need the machine."

"I do all my work by hand," I assured her. I had watched Tante Eloise ply her needle, and if she could do so, so could I.

"You're *sure*, Gabriella? I don't want Katie's underslip ruined."

I crossed my heart. "Have no fear."

She found me the fine flouncy underslip she had cut out and sewed up for her granddaughter, found me the lace and the sewing basket, and I settled myself in the big cozy chair in front of the stove in the parlor, with the homely little goblin cat on the arm of the chair and the ancestral Shevalas in their picture frames looking down. *Don't worry,* I said, to disarm them, *I can do it.* And thus I began.

Luckily, I found a threaded needle in the sewing basket. I took it up in my right hand and took up underslip and lace in the left. Tante Eloise had always begun sewing from underneath; I did this, too. I summoned to mind exactly what she looked like, exactly what she had done on those days when she'd sat on my cot in the damp ugly basement, redesigning my charity-box clothes. She had squinted her eyes, screwed up her nose, and said, *Tsk! Tsk! Tsk!* as she moved along, her needle taking tiny little stitches. I screwed up my nose, squinted my eyes, and said, *Tsk! Tsk! Tsk!* as I did the same.

When Mama came in, she looked impressed.

"You can trust me," I said.

"Gabriella, this is a great help."

I gave her my sunniest.

The moment she left the room, I ran into trouble. My thread came out of the needle, I lost the needle in the folds of the underslip, then I stuck my thumb on a new needle as I tried to thread it, and I left tiny blood stains on the fine lace that Mama herself had tatted. Only thoughts of Missouri and of being put into an institution kept me going. An hour and a half of utter frustration went by, and as I was taking the final stitch, ready to snip the last thread, Mama Shevala returned. I lifted the lacy underslip to show her all I'd done, only to find . . . I'd sewed the underslip to the skirt of the dress I was wearing.

Mama's mouth turned down. "Oh, my dear . . ."

"It's nothing, really nothing . . ."

"Look here, you've ruined it."

"Oh, no, it isn't ruined."

I winged a prayer heavenward, asking for a miracle, but got none.

"*Gabriella.*" Mama's shoulders sagged. "I don't know what to do with you. I just don't know."

My shoulders sagged, too. I could have cried, but what was the use? The institution drew nearer and nearer. I would die there.

Mama pressed her lips into a hard white line. The wisp of stray curl came down from her comb; she ignored it. "Gabriella, how have you managed all these years? You can't do anything at all. How do you expect to get along? You've lied to me, you've lied to poor old Papa Joe, you've lied to everyone. You're not any kind of chore girl. You ought to be ashamed." The mild blue eyes showed no mercy. "Hear me? *Ashamed.*"

"I *am*. I am ashamed." This boiled up out of my

depths. "I want to do things, but I don't know how. No one would ever let me, or teach me. I'm not really a chore girl, I can't cook, or sew or clean. I don't know the first thing about horses, or how to milk a cow. I've never even seen a real chicken. I'm sorry and ashamed, but I didn't mean to lie. I just did." I averted my face so she couldn't see I was dying inside.

When I'd finished, she said, "Gabriella, I feel so sorry for you, I truly do. I wish I could help you somehow, but there's nothing I can do. When Katherine comes for the children, you will have to go. We can't afford to keep you. If it weren't for the children, we'd let you go now."

"I understand."

"I am glad that you do understand, Gabriella. But, before you go I want to teach you how to use a needle—it's the least I can do. So far you've ruined everything you've touched, but see here . . . see these stitches, see how small they are, how even? It's possible you have a natural bent for sewing. Now, let's save what we can of the lace, try to save the underslip . . ." She heaved a sigh and started in with a razor, cutting the stitches I'd worked so hard to put in, to free the underslip from my dress. ". . . I truly believe you can learn, Gabriella, but you must promise never to lie to me again."

"Cross my heart and hope to die. I swear it on a thousand Bibles, on a hundred thousand Bibles . . ."

"One is enough, Gabriella."

As it worked out, I did have a natural bent for sewing. I learned to thread a needle, how to hold the edges of fabrics together, how to fasten the thread without tying a knot, and many other sewing secrets. As her Christmas gift to me, Mama promised to teach me darning and mending, "and then if you wish,

122

you may go on to embroidery. If we have time, I will teach you to knit. And if we have time, I will show you how to run the machine. *If,* I say. Nothing's for certain."

When I pointed out that my legs would never reach the pedal to run the machine, she said I must not encourage such a negative attitude. "Never say die, Gabriella. You never know what you can do until you set your mind to do it."

I had already set my mind to something much harder than sewing: I had decided to grow.

As marvelous as Mama's gift was for me, Papa Joe promised he had something for me that would be even better. "It will change your life forever," he told me that evening when he'd come in from the milking. "I'm going to give you your true heart's desire."

Katie and Charles overheard this promise. They climbed onto his lap as he sat by the fire, teasing him to get him to give up his secret, but he would not. "Tomorrow," he said. "It is coming by a special delivery."

"Papa Joe," Katie cried, "the snow is too deep. It's already covered the lane, and the roads will be drifted so that nothing can be delivered tomorrow."

Charles had changed into his yellow pajamas and was almost asleep in Papa Joe's arms. He studied his grandfather with serious eyes. "If Papa Joe says it will be here tomorrow, it'll be here tomorrow, because he never lies. I can't wait for tomorrow."

I was not as trusting as Charles. Papa Joe's idea of my "true heart's desire" could be anything. I thought of the little dwarf man he'd promised me and I feared the worst.

Christmas Day the Shevalas were up and in full swing by six A.M. Mama was in the kitchen stuffing dressing into the nude, dimpled carcass of a goose. Tasha bustled to and fro, setting out the china and singing carols in a high soprano voice. I had never seen her so animated. She even said good morning to me. As for the children, they had already made several trips up to my room, urging me to come to see what Santa Claus had left in my stocking. When I argued that I hadn't hung a stocking, they insisted that someone had hung a stocking with my name on it. "And it's stuffed!" Charles said. He and Katie had tugged on my arm until I gave up and came downstairs to look.

I'd never had a Christmas stocking before. In fact, I had never had Christmas. My parents, bless them, never held with celebrations, nor had my dear aunts. When I went downstairs at six that morning, all my senses were overwhelmed. I felt as giddy as a ten-year-old and hardly knew where to turn first. I hobbled to the kitchen, to the parlor, back again, taking in the fragrance of sage and peppermint, the sound of Tasha's *alleluias*, the glitter of tinsel Papa Joe had strung at all the windows, and—most wonderful of all!—the Christmas tree glowing in one corner of the parlor. Beside it hung a brown woolen stocking with my name on it.

Charles stood by impatiently. "Take it down," he said. "See what's in it. Katie and I got candy and nuts, and *presents*."

"You'll have presents, too," Katie said. "Look and see."

My hands were shaking so that I could hardly take the stocking from its hook. The room had grown overwarm from the blazing wood fire in the stove, though outside snow piled up against the windows and the wind was howling in the chimney. Goblin wound himself in and out between my ankles and my crutches, while I struggled to free the stocking.

"Here," Katie said, "let me do it." She got the stocking off its hook and gave it to me. Inside were all the treats I'd always seen in candy store windows and had longed for. There were old-fashioned chocolate drops, bright pillows of hard Christmas candy, walnuts in the shell, sticks of peppermint, chewy orange slices, and down in the toe of the sock I found a perfect orange. And something else . . . I thrust my arm deeper to pull a package out. It had been wrapped in white tissue paper, tied with red ribbon, and a small Christmas tag read: TO GABRIELLA, FROM SANTA. I put the stocking down to concentrate on the package. Inside, there were small wooden figures, carved and painted with obvious care. A pair of peacocks, an elephant the size of my fist, a small spotted horse, and a little sleigh containing three tiny people: Papa Joe had made them all.

"Look, they're us!" Katie lifted the sleigh on the palm of her hand, and I saw that she was right. A little boy with yellow hair and a bright red muffler had to be Charles. "And this is you, Gabriella, and this one with the stocking cap is me." She carried them to the window and held them up to the scant winter light.

As pleased as I was with the delicate figures, I had nothing to say; I'd stuffed three chocolate drops and a large piece of hard peppermint candy into my mouth and could not speak. Having lived a life of restriction, I craved sweetness, and I would have embarrassed myself, the way I made a pig of myself with the candy, if anyone had been paying attention. It seemed as though I could never get enough, and the stocking seemed unending. I discovered peanut brittle, fudge squares wrapped in tinfoil, toffee, candy-coated nuts. Tante Eloise would have thought me disgraceful. But who cared about Tante Eloise? Not me. I popped two more chocolates into my mouth and forgot her.

It was a perfect day. Small gifts were exchanged and I found myself richer by two embroidered hankies, a bookmark from Katie, a small hand mirror from Charles, a string of glass beads from Tasha (which surprised me), and nothing from Ambrose (which didn't surprise me). For my part, I entertained them with a dramatized reading of "Snowbound," by Whittier, which everyone claimed to enjoy—except Ambrose, who sneered.

After the Christmas dinner, Papa Joe said he was ready to give me my surprise.

"But the little carved figures," I said, "weren't they my surprise? I don't deserve anything more, surely?"

"You didn't deserve that much," said Ambrose, and Papa Joe kicked him in the shin. As Ambrose grabbed his leg and grimaced, Papa Joe said, "Come on outside. The present has arrived. Oh, but you are going to love it, little woman. See if you don't."

From the closet under the stairs, I took out the jacket the trainman had given me, put on a bright knitted cap that had once belonged to the children's mother, found a pair of mismatched mittens, tucked my crutches under my arms, and went out through the kitchen and the milk porch, followed by the children and the farm dog. Goblin had run ahead, out into the snow, behind Papa Joe. Goblin's long skimpy tail stuck straight up, then curled at the tip like a question mark. The cat hated the cold and shook his paws at every step.

"Well?" Papa Joe demanded, when we had gathered in the yard in front of the house. "What do you think? Do you like it?"

126

All I could think was, *there must be some mistake.*

"A horse?" Katie said.

"Not for Gabriella," Mama said, her teeth chattering with cold. "Surely, not for Gabriella."

Ambrose muttered something obscene and ran back into the house.

"It isn't a horse," Papa Joe said, his breath a white cloud. "It's a pony."

It was a black-and-white pony, identical to the pony I had found in my stocking. Beside it stood a small black sleigh with a gilt design painted on its sides, and long curved runners. The black-and-white pony turned its head to look at us, jingling brass sleigh bells as it did so.

"For me, Papa Joe? It couldn't be for me."

Papa Joe's arms dropped to his sides. Large square snowflakes settled on his lashes. "You don't like her."

"Oh, but I do." I couldn't bear to hurt him. "I like her, I do." *For me? A horse? A horse was my true heart's desire?* "I like her very much." *How could I take a horse back to Missouri? Could I take her into the institution?*

The pony tossed her mane and made a low blowing sound through her nostrils, then rubbed her black-and-white head against the inside of a black-and-white foreleg. Small brass bells jingled at each movement, neat ears pricked forward, a neat black hoof pawed at the snow on the ground. She was tied to the hitch rail with a rope, which Papa Joe had started untying.

At this the children sprang to life. "Can we ride her?" Katie asked, jumping up and down. Charles climbed into the sleigh. "Take us for a ride," he shouted. His cheeks had turned bright red from the cold, and his stocking cap had slipped down so far it almost covered his eyes. The cat leaped into the sleigh beside him, yowling lustily. Charles cracked an imaginary whip. "Giddy up! Let's go!"

"Gabriella first," Papa Joe said. "Gabriella gets to ride first, because this pony belongs to her." He thrust my crutches upright in a snowbank and swooped me up and onto the pony's back. I took a gulp of cold air before the pony stepped forward to follow Papa Joe. Too terrified to speak, I motioned that I *had* to get off. Papa Joe stood beside me, grinning. "I told you you would love it, little woman. Oh, but you look *grand*."

My teeth rattled in my mouth like bones, from cold, from terror. I grabbed onto the pony's coarse mane as she walked along beside Papa Joe. Even so, I lost my balance and started to fall. Papa Joe caught me. Steadying me with his arm, pushing me back into place, he said, "Let's go down the lane and back. Oh, but you look grand. If only the Halvorsons could see me now, wouldn't they be green? Just wait till we show you off at the fair! How the people are going to love you!"

In spite of a lifelong devotion to the story of *Black Beauty*, I wasn't ready for this. The pony's back was broad and slippery, and my legs stuck out at awkward angles. Each step she took sent me sliding to one side or the other. The ground was so far below me I couldn't see it, except for vague whiteness. My stomach rose up in my throat, my head lurched; I had no more fear of being sent back to Missouri, however, for I knew I wouldn't live much longer. I could hear my bones snapping and breaking as I imagined myself hitting the ground. My neck would break, my skull would squash like a pumpkin. With fear and trembling, I turned to Papa Joe, desperate to get off the pony. I looked at his face, and with a sudden realization, saw that I was on a level with him. Mounted on the pony, I was almost as tall as he. Tall. I was *tall.*

"Well?" he asked. "Shall we keep her?"

Without a hesitation I knew the answer. "I can't live without her."

One trip down the lane and back and I learned to keep my balance. As we started once more to return to the sleigh, where the children sat watching and cheering me on, I pressed my heels into the pony's barrel sides, and Princess stepped out in a quick little walk. I pressed my heels harder, and she started to jog. Shep ran alongside, wagging his flag of a tail and barking.

"Hey!" Papa Joe pulled back on the lead rope. "Didn't anyone tell you, my treasure, that you have to learn to walk before you can run?" Clusters of snowflakes glistened on his hat. His black eyes shone. "Tomorrow you can start driving the sleigh. When you've learned to do that you can go anywhere you want."

"Can I go alone?"

"As soon as you're ready, not a minute sooner."

He had been right about one thing: Princess, the name I picked for the pony, was the answer to my fondest hope. Because of her, I could become independent. I could live a life of my own, not the lives that happened in books, not the lives that other people lived—my own. It had started with him, Timothy. Knowing I was loved, I could do anything.

Perched awkwardly on the back of the pony, slipping this way and that, bouncing up and down, lurching, terrified of falling, I raised one mittened hand to catch the falling snowflakes. Grand as I felt at that moment, they could have been galaxies of burning stars.

# 12

The children had two weeks for Christmas vacation, a time that all of us attempted to savor to the fullest. Mama cooked all their favorite meals, Tasha taught them to dance the mazurka, Papa Joe invented outlandish pranks for them, while I simply hugged them at every opportunity and read to them from my best-loved books. At night I cried. And it wasn't just that they were going away, but that I was going, too.

I packed my suitcase, packed my carton, asked Papa Joe for a second carton to pack the overflow from carton number one. He left it as I'd asked, upstairs in my room, with a roll of binders' twine to make it fast; when I found it there, I cried and cried. At last I dug out the calling card that Timothy had given me, and I addressed a letter to him. It took two full days to write the letter:

Dearest friend,

Due to an unforeseen circumstance of fate, I shall be leaving the area soon. As you mentioned that you would like to come again to pay me a visit, I do not want you to arrive at the farm and find me gone, not with what the price of gas has become. I am sorry that we will not meet again, for your visit meant so much to me. We have so very much in common. If you know any prayers for someone living in an institution, I hope you'll say one of those prayers for me, as that is where I shall be living. Some institutions can be very modern and progressive, or so I've heard. Some are very much like a real home. I hope that that is what I'll find.

If you are so inclined to answer, you may write to me here at the Shevala farm. Mama has promised to forward my mail as soon as I have an address. Until then, I remain your faithful friend,

Gabriella Wheeler.

I prayed that he would answer before I left. I prayed that he would drop everything and come to see me. I knew he cared for me: His kiss had proved that.

Once I had written the letter, when I was sure I'd gotten it exactly right—not too backward, not too bold—I had to find some way to get it down the hill to the mailbox. Usually, it was Ambrose who went down to the mail. Obviously, I could not ask *him* to take it for me. At last I decided to ask Tasha. After all, she and I both harbored the same kind of secret. But Tasha had hardly ever volunteered to speak to me, and it took courage for me to ask her for this favor. Then when I did ask, she looked at me blankly. "You want me to carry a letter down to the mailbox? You want me to make a special trip down the hill, in all this snow, just to . . ." She shot a dark look at me and then at the address on the envelope. A knowing expression replaced her indignation. She narrowed her dark eyes slyly. "Ah-ha," she said, "I see how the land lays."

"Then you'll do it?"

"Of course not." She gave me a scornful look and tossed her black hair over one slim shoulder, rattling her beads and her earrings. "Why should I put myself out for *you*?"

"Because," I said warmly, "I am not the only one who has a secret, Tasha." I could be every bit as sly, if driven to it.

For once she looked flustered. "You mean . . . you know?"

"About you and the Halvorson boy? I won't tell, though of course I really should tell. It's wicked to deceive . . ." I loved the mystery, the daring, the secret guilt, the power I held in my hands.

Tasha's whole demeanor changed, her haughtiness dissolving into sudden tears, which she tried to hold back. "Gabriella, promise you won't tattle . . . Ambrose will kill me. Promise you won't tell anyone at all, *please*."

I could see that she would be glad to walk to the mailbox every day thereafter, if I asked her to. With no further argument, she pulled on her galoshes, bundled up in her warm outdoor clothes, and went out to mail my letter. I wasn't proud of what I'd done, but I had to get a message to Timothy if I ever wanted to see him again, and oh! I did—I did!

Happily, I would not have to resort to such blackmail again, because—as promised—Papa Joe started teaching me to drive the pony and sleigh. "A skill once learned is never lost," he said, when I pointed out that I would be leaving soon. The children's mother was expected any minute. "Besides," he added with a private wink in my direction, "that daughter of mine, that Katherine, has never been noted for keeping her promises."

We were standing in the spiced and steamy kitchen, putting on our wraps, to go out to the horse barn to harness the pony when this conversation took place. Goblin was winding around and around my crutches and legs; the children were well out of earshot. The significance of what Papa Joe had just said took me aback. "You mean . . . ? Do you mean they might not go away? Their mother might not come for them?"

He winked again. "If I had a dime for every promise she's broken, I'd be rich as a Swede today."

If Charles hadn't come to me at that moment, asking me to help him buckle his boots and tie his stocking cap under his chin, I would have questioned Papa Joe more. As it was, I didn't want to talk about the children's mother in front of them. They loved her, that was plain. However much I didn't want them to leave with her, I also didn't want them to suffer disappointment. Ever since Christmas they had both been counting the days, not certain if she would arrive before school took up again, hoping she would.

In spite of myself, I hoped she wouldn't.

Every afternoon, after sewing, when the cold spread blue shadows across wind-rifted fields of snow, Papa Joe, the children, and I hitched Princess to the sleigh and took turns driving down the lane. Papa Joe said that Princess was too rambunctious for Katie or Charles to drive her alone. "On top of that," he said, "the pony belongs to Gabriella. What Gabriella says, the pony has to do."

And Princess was willing, even though I sometimes gave the wrong signals. Sometimes I wasn't sure what I should tell her to do. I knew I should slap the long leather driving reins lightly against her back to get her to go forward, or go faster. I knew I should pull back on the reins—but gently!—to get her to stop. Pull left to go left, pull right to go right. But what should I do when the sleigh runners hit a chunk of ice, sending the sleigh out of the track, thrusting it into a steep bank of snow, where it stuck fast?

The others had waited at the start of the lane, near the hitch rail. I could see them, as if at a distance, behind the scrim of falling snow. I would have to solve this problem myself. I slapped the reins to tell Princess to go. She could not move forward. I pulled the reins to the right, but the snowbank was too high for her to draw the sleigh over it. I pulled to the left . . . no use. She turned her head around to face me, her ears flat, and gave me a long disgusted look. She lifted her lip and showed me her teeth.

I did not like the looks of this at all. "You have to do what I say, Princess."

She gave me a laugh.

Meanwhile the snow fell thicker and faster. I couldn't see Papa Joe or the children at all. The farm dog had stayed behind with them, so I couldn't send him to bring back help. When I looked over the side of the sleigh toward the ground, I saw that the runners were about six inches above the snow, that the front curl of the runners had slid into a dip, before sticking in the bank. With little but a half-baked plan in mind, I whipped the reins around the crosspiece designed to hold them, left my crutches where they lay on the floor in front of the driving seat, and climbed out of the sleigh, stepping down onto the runner. Princess turned her head again and whickered.

A colder wind spun down from the distant mountains, picking up whirlpools of the soft new snow, spinning them away. "Don't worry, Princess. I know what I'm doing." I didn't, but Princess couldn't guess the truth. If she was ever going to trust me, I'd have to be the one to get the sleigh free. The snow fell so thickly now that only the pony's black patches were visible against the falling white curtains of snow. Cold bit through my thin stockings.

Clinging with both hands to the side of the sleigh, I inched my way along the metal runner until I was teetering at the very end. I never have weighed very much, but I weighed just enough that afternoon so that the sleigh's runners dropped to the ground, and the sleigh itself was free. It fell to the ground with a soft thud, a sound just loud enough to start Princess into a gentle trot, then a faster, harder trot. If I hadn't had such a firm grip on the back of the sleigh by that time I would have been thrown to one side and knocked senseless, at the very least.

Princess was cold, tired, and highly annoyed at all she'd been through. She quickened her pace, the sleigh singing along behind her, with me still on the runner, hanging on for dear life. I was still in this position when we approached the end of the lane. As familiar landmarks sped by, I heard Papa Joe shout for Princess to stop, but Princess did not. She had gone from a trot into a gallop. The sleigh swayed dangerously across the packed snow of the lane, scaring me so that I couldn't even call out or wave as we sped past the children and Papa Joe. When old Shep joined us, barking along behind the pony's heels, Princess went faster, through the open gate into the farmyard, and she zipped straight through the wide barn doors and into the barn. The sleigh went in with her, with me clinging to the side, too scared to let go.

Papa Joe came running in his long-legged, loose-jointed stride, and behind him came Katie and Charles. "Ah, my little woman, what a fine show you put on," Papa Joe cried. He loosened my frozen grip on the sleigh and boosted me up on his shoulder, while I was still too cold and too scared to protest. "Ah, won't it be grand when we take you to the fair?"

"Gabriella, are you all right?" Katie asked. "Papa Joe, put her down, she's scared."

"Scared?" He laughed. "This one's scared of nothing. You saw what she did. Came riding by us like a circus act, that's what. Oh, she's got talent, talent to spare. What a sensation she's going to be. Just wait until Halvorson gets a load of *this*. Won't he turn green? Just wait." Papa Joe set me down on a bale of hay, while he set about unhitching the sleigh, taking off the pony's harness, making her fast, rubbing her down.

"Papa Joe," Katie said, drawing herself up to full height. "I love you, I really do, but sometimes you can be so *mean*."

Papa Joe did not respond to this, whether because he hadn't heard her accusation, or because he was busy removing the bit from the pony's mouth, I don't know. But I heard, and hearing what I had only thought to myself made my eyes sting. Why did I have to be a circus act to be valued? Why couldn't Papa Joe value me for myself? It seemed such a simple thing. If it hadn't been for my faith in my brown-eyed young man, and if it hadn't been for the children, I would have believed myself abjectly unlovable. But I had my memory of him, and I had Charles and Katie winding their arms around me, asking if I was warm enough, if I was scared, and telling me over and over how worried they'd been when they saw the sleigh fly by without me in it.

Katie ran to fetch my crutches, and Charles sat on the hay bale beside me. "We love you bestest of anybody, Gabriella, except our mother—of course. Children have to love their mother best. I think it's a law."

I thought of my own mother, quiet and dark within her darkened parlor, her bitterness, her unrewarded life, and I wondered if she could see me now. If she was looking down from some heavenly cloud or other, what did she think? Would she want her only child to be a circus act? Did she care at all? Probably not. She had washed her hands of me the day she'd discovered exactly what I was.

That night at the supper table I had to listen as Papa Joe bragged about my sleigh ride, about my skill and daring. Ambrose, who had been silent through the meat and potatoes, frowning at his plate, twitching his mustache, gave me a long sardonic stare over the hot apple pie. "If Gabriella is such a little wonder, Papa Joe, why not put her to work now? She'll be gone before too long. Let's get some work out of her while she's here. Let her pay off some board and room."

I did not point out that I had finished all of the backed-up mending, that I had darned dozens of pairs of hole-ridden Shevala socks—many of them his—that I was learning to run the sewing machine and had turned ten flour sacks into hemmed and bleached tea towels, ready for cross-stitch embroidery, which I personally would see to—as soon as I learned how to do it. I sat there with my napkin around my neck, hoping Mama would defend me. She did not.

"Work?" said Papa Joe. "What do you mean—work?"

"Work," Ambrose sneered. "Maybe you've heard of it."

"What kind of work?" Mama asked.

"If she's so hot with a horse and sleigh," said Ambrose, "she might as well drive the kids to school. I, for one, am sick of doing it. Back and forth, back and forth, every day the same. I say let her do it. She's got nothing else to do with her time."

Charles clapped his hands above his head. "Hooray! Let Gabriella drive us. Ambrose is always such a grouch."

"Not such a bad idea," said Papa Joe. He rubbed his stubbled chin. "What do you think, little woman? It might keep you in practice, you'll be ready for the fair."

"I would like that very much," I said, summoning what dignity I could. "Nothing gives more satisfaction than being useful."

With this began a new facet of my chore girl career.

By the time the children's Christmas vacation had ended, Princess and I were seasoned friends. She never ran away with me again, she forgave my ignorance, and she seemed genuinely glad to see me whenever I went out to the horse barn to see her. On my part, I learned to treat her with as much consideration and respect as she deserved.

When Papa Joe, or Katie, or Charles were in her stall with her, she would move about freely, munching hay, nuzzling her visitors, pushing the cat around with her nose. But as soon as I entered her box stall, knee-deep in bedding straw, and teetering on my crutches because of the uneven plank floor, Princess would stand stock-still, letting me come up to her, instead of the other way. It was as if she understood how fragile I was compared to the others, and she was taking every precaution not to injure me. In the time it took for me to learn how to drive her properly, I learned how loving and gentle she could be. She had large dark eyes, a velvet black nose, and a black coat with large white patches—continents of white afloat in a midnight sea.

On Monday morning, we got up and dressed in the dark, ate a hot breakfast by lantern light, and went out to the sleigh long before sunup. Papa Joe had harnessed the pony and had her waiting by the hitching post with the sleigh. He had heated up bricks for the bucket to warm us on our journey. The air was dark and ringing cold. Princess pranced in place, ready for adventure. Her small ears pricked forward and back; she wanted to go. Sleigh bells rippled a brassy music. High in the sky, the whitest of moons floated free of a cloud.

The children climbed in beside me. I gathered up the reins and released the holding brake, prepared to take off, when Papa Joe came running back out of the house. "Hey! Little woman! I've got a present for you. Don't go off without your present."

I made Princess wait, while Papa Joe climbed onto the sleigh. "Your shapka! Your head will freeze and with it your brains if you leave without your shapka."

Onto my head he placed a tall fur hat exactly like his own. It was wonderfully warm pulled down around my ears, and I knew it made me look taller. I slapped the reins lightly against the pony's back. She started out with a quick little trot, the sleigh singing along behind her, lighted by moonlight.

139

With Papa Joe, I had made the run to Bad Horse School several times and no misadventure. Even with this experience, however, I had no confidence that I could do it alone as we started out that morning. At least this was the case until we had arrived at the bottom of the long Shevala hill and stopped at the mailboxes, "just in case."

Katie climbed out of the sleigh, and to my joy, to my surprise, she brought back a letter addressed to me. Princess pawed at the snow and tossed her head, but I made her stand until I'd read the letter:

My dearest Gabriella,
You must not speak of institutions. If worse comes to worst, let me know. I will do what I can. Keep me posted. Remember, you are loved.

Timothy Brentwood

Loved. He'd said it again: I was loved.

If Timothy loved me I could do anything. With the moon shining full upon it, the letter in my hand glowed as if with white fire. It could have been a traveler's stove, for the warmth it gave me.

Katie sat beside me. "We better hurry, Gabriella, or we'll be late."

I stuffed the letter into my pocket, where it warmed me better than my coat. Princess flicked her ears, I gave her her head, and we started smartly into the dark piney forest, following the moonlit road toward the school. Hat on my head, letter in my pocket, work to be done, it seemed as though all my prayers had been answered. For all my experience, I still had not learned how quickly and whimsically He can change his mind; the journey had scarcely begun.

# 13

Every weekday morning went the same. I drove the children to the schoolhouse, turned around in the yard, and drove the pony and sleigh home again. There was a pony barn beside the school, and if either of the children had been old enough to drive the sleigh, Princess could have been stabled in the pony barn until the return trip home. Or I could have stayed at the school, if it hadn't been that I was needed at the farm. I had made myself needed.

*You are loved* had given me a sense of confidence and fire. I had taken to sewing like a trout to a stream, and I'd learned to clean—clean anything: cookstove, dishes, walls, floors, windows. There was simply no end to my energy or usefulness. Mama couldn't get over it. "I almost hope Katherine doesn't come back.

141

I don't know what happened to you, Gabriella. You're a wonder! It must be that pony and sleigh. What a cruel trick it was of Papa Joe to give them to you. You'll have to leave them here when you go. At least the sewing, you've learned to do that. Whatever happens, a woman needs to know how to sew."

Not even this could bring down my high spirits. From the time I returned in the morning until it was time to ride to the school in the later afternoon, I worked, worked hard, and had never been happier. Of course I had written straight back to Timothy and had been able to mail the letter myself, placing it in the letter box with the red flag up to signal the mailman. Then came the long wait, the expectation, the muttered prayers and charms as I stopped the sleigh on those dark snowy mornings, with the glow of knowing I was loved to warm me from the inside out like a traveler's stove. Day after day the box was empty.

A month had gone and there had been no word from the children's mother. Katie had come down to breakfast on several different mornings, her eyes red from crying. "I hate her," she told me on one such occasion. "I hate her so much I can't even talk about it. Our father died, then she took us to live in Spokane, and then she met this *person,* so she sent us here to live with Mama and Papa Joe. It's been a year now. She keeps saying she'll come for us, then she doesn't. I hate her so much, Gabriella. Is it true you go straight to the devil if you say you hate somebody?"

Charles took a bite of his oatmeal and gave his sister a long level look. "You can't say those things about Mama. She promised she'd come sometime after Christmas, and she will. She loves us, and she wouldn't lie."

"I don't believe her," Katie said. "I hate her. She never cares about anybody's feelings. She just does what she wants and then expects us to fall in with her plans. Even if she does come to get us, I'm not going back. I'd rather stay here with Gabriella. She's always nice. She never makes promises and then doesn't keep them."

I mulled this over as I drove the children to school that morning. I had almost stopped worrying about what would happen to me when Katie and Charles left, for it had begun to appear that Papa Joe was right: Their mother wasn't going to come for them. Also I'd developed my chore girl skills to prove myself to Mama, so she would let me stay on. And then there was Timothy. He'd never let them put me into an institution. Whatever happened, I counted on him to save me. His word was gold.

Strong winds had drifted snow across the narrow country road that led to the Bad Horse school. In the moonlight it shone like wind-sculpted stone, making a bright smooth surface for the sleigh. We sped along behind the pony, her mane flung out, harness bells ringing, her small hard hooves trotting a steady rhythm against the crusty snow. The moon skimmed along above us, behind us, over our shoulders, slipping through the ragged trees, a white bird on a silver string.

After Katie's outburst, none of us had felt like talking, until suddenly Charles said to me, "Isn't this wonderful, the moon and the dark and the snow?" He was sitting on my left, sharing the bearskin rug with his sister and me. "As long as I live I will always remember this ride." He waited a moment, his face tight with worry. "Do people remember things after they die?"

"What a question," I said, while forest and moon

and snowdrifts sped by. "People your age don't have to worry about questions like that."

"I like to be prepared," he said.

"Oh, don't mind him," Katie cut in. "He's always like this. Ever since our father died he's been morbid."

"I'm not morbid," Charles snapped. "I just want to know, that's all."

"Well, you can't know. Nobody knows." Katie's attack seemed unusually vicious. "So stop asking questions."

Charles's small body pressed tight against my side. The pompon on his stocking cap bounced gaily up and down, but I'd become increasingly aware of how small he was, how scared, how vulnerable, how unfairly he and Katie had been treated. I wanted to put my arms around both of them, to protect them against every danger. When the sleigh pulled into the wide moonlit drive that curved out of the denseness of forest and into the open field where the schoolhouse stood, stern and steep-sided as an old-fashioned teacher, I had to whoa the pony to a stop and let the children climb out.

Golden light shone out of the schoolhouse windows. The door opened, and the teacher gave me a friendly wave. Katie had told me before that their teacher wanted to meet me, that she thought I was a "remarkable young woman," to use Katie's words, and wouldn't I *please* come in. For just the briefest of moments I considered tying Princess to the post in front of the building and going inside; I missed books, discussions, the atmosphere of learning. But then I envisioned myself walking into a room full of gawking staring children and I decided to return to the farm as always. I'd had my fill of being laughed at, stared at, of being treated like a circus freak. I did not want to be a "remarkable young woman." I wanted to be ordinary, like everybody else. I wanted to be loved for my ordinary qualities—not for my exceptions.

With the bucket of bricks to warm my feet, the porter's jacket to warm my shoulders, the bearskin rug snug across my lap, the black fur cap sitting tall on my head, and with Timothy's letter still in my pocket, I turned the pinto toward home. I had never felt safer, more needed, more proud of my accomplishments. I could not have known that something was to happen that would change these feelings drastically.

Whether it was remembering Charles's strange question, or whether by instinct, or by some inner terror of my own, I'll never know, but it seemed to me that danger lurked on every side as I started my return trip through the forest. I found myself sitting forward on the slatted seat, tense, listening, peering into the dark of the thickets, trying to see what lay waiting. To give myself courage I tried to whistle. I'd never been good at whistling, and now the effect was macabre. I gave up the whistling and started to sing, off-key but with determination, a hymn we had sung at the academy: "Lord of all faithfulness . . ."

Princess's ears flicked forward and back, the white tips two jots of light against the gloom. She was as scared as I was and shied nervously at every change in scene, a fallen log at the edge of the road, a strangely shaped or bent tree, the shadow the moon made on its trip through the forest. What had once been lovely now appeared as a threat. I could still have turned back, but I didn't; I went on.

When we had gone a mile or so from the school, another two miles and we'd be safe at the farm, a single shadow slipped out of the dark beneath the trees and then slipped in again. And there were more shadows waiting. Princess leaned heavily into her harness. She put her ears flat and broke into a run. The sleigh bells rang out in a panic. The sleigh lurched this way and that as I hauled back on the reins to slow the pony, but I din't have the strength to stop her. My face was burned by bitter air; I was blinded by speed. Behind us I heard galloping hoofbeats and men's shouts.

With the pinto in flight, the sleigh fanned to the left, to the right, and I lost the reins. Chunks of snow and ice flew back from the pony's hooves, hitting me in the face. I grabbed onto the carved wooden brace and held on for my life. Desperate, I reached for the hand brake, grabbed it, pulled it sharply back, and the sleigh shot across the icy surface of the road, jolted to a stop, and I flew forward, pitched over the side and into a deep drift of snow. For a moment or so I thought I was dead, but then I heard Princess whinny in distress. I wanted to call to her but my fall had stunned me so I couldn't make a sound. I lay where I was, too scared and shocked to move.

I became aware of the presence of horses, then booted feet. A dark voice shouted, "Hey? What is this? Where is he?"

"There," another shouted. "Over there, stuck in the snow. Grab him by the ears, haul him out."

"We'll teach him a lesson he'll never forget!"

Strong arms raised me up out of the snowbank. They lifted me up like a floppy rag doll. There was a shocked silence, then my tormentor gasped and gave a nervous laugh. The day had grown lighter, but it was still too dark for me to see their faces clearly. Now they were all laughing, six or seven of them, laughing nervously at first, but gaining strength as they looked at what they'd caught.

146

"What is it?" The man who held me up by the back of my jacket was the size and disposition of an ogre. As I started to come to my senses I aimed a kick at his groin. This only made him laugh harder, and he held me out at arm's length, though I struggled and flailed to get down.

"Whatever it is," said another, "it sure isn't Ambrose."

"It's nothin' like Ambrose."

"It's that little dwarf they keep on the farm."

I swung my fist at my kidnapper's jaw, which only made him laugh—a loud coarse laugh—before he dropped me in the snow. I tried to stand but fell over. I looked around for my crutches. They were nowhere in sight. From a short distance I heard Princess calling, and it hurt me when I couldn't go to her to help her. She could have been injured, could have broken a leg; anything could have happened and I couldn't get to her. In a rage I struggled to my feet. "Get out of here!" I shouted at the men. "Leave me alone!"

"Look," one of them squawked, "it talks. The Bohunk talks."

"I'm not a *Bohunk*."

They were still no more than shadows. One of them came up behind me and pushed me hard. When I fell my hat went flying. "It's got to be a Bohunk!" he shouted. "Look at the Bohunk hat!"

A voice I hadn't heard before spoke up in my defense. "Leave her alone. It's Ambrose you're after. This little dwarf girl is nothing like Ambrose. Leave her alone."

"Aw, shut up, Olmstead. We ain't doin' nothin' . . . not yet." A burst of laughter followed this remark, and the chill that clamped down on my body had nothing to do with the weather. The men had formed a circle around me, having dismounted and left their horses with a member of their group. The men were like giants to me, dark and ogreish in the turgid light.

"We could have some fun with her."

"Who would ever know?"

"Ambrose."

A roar of laughter followed this remark.

"What will he do when he finds out we been fooling around with his girl?"

"He'd have to fight us then. He couldn't back out."

I started to back away across the crusted snow, but the nearest one swooped down on me, lifted my head by my hair, and then shoved my face down hard into the snow. "How do you like that, Bohunk? Want me to do it again? Hunh?"

"No . . . don't . . ." The pain was terrible. I felt as though my face had been stripped of flesh in the grainy snow. "No . . ." As much as that hurt, it was nothing compared to the rage that came boiling up from inside me. I got to my feet, tottering, and swung my fists, but the tears poured down so hot and thick I was blinded and struck nothing but air. I stumbled, fell forward, shouting at them in rage, "You're going to be sorry for this, all of you! Oh, boy, are you going to pay!"

I believe I could have killed them—if I'd managed to get my hands on them. Before I could do any damage, one of them grabbed me around the waist, from behind, and lifted me high up over his head. Trees spun around at the edge of my vision. Princess and the upended sleigh went around in a whirl. If I fell I'd break every bone in my body. And I could plainly see I was going to fall. They would hide my

148

body in the forest, where no one would find me till spring. I'd never see Timothy again. I kicked and flailed and screamed, but no use. My every protest was met with mocking laughter. *Oh, God,* I thought, *get ready for me now. Here I come.*

# 14

"Leave her alone."

"*What?*"

Beneath me the ground stopped spinning. The giant who'd been holding me swung around. "What was that, Olmstead? What did you say?"

"You heard me. I said, put her down. Gently." His voice was light but held authority. He went on, "You came out here to beat up on Ambrose, and this isn't Ambrose. It's that little girl who works for Turkey Joe. She's never hurt nobody, so I say put her down and get out of here before somebody comes along. Leave her alone."

The giant set me down on the ground by his feet. I would've grabbed his leg and sunk my teeth in but he was wearing boots, so I doubled my fist and slugged him as hard as I could. He paid no attention. I slugged him again and again, but he didn't seem to notice. If I'd had a gun I'd have shot him. He was making obscene remarks, alluding to my virginity and what I might have been doing out here in the woods. At this, Olmstead hit him and he paid attention. There was a scuffle, more insults, a few blows exchanged. Meanwhile, the others had mounted their horses and were slinking back into the forest.

"*Bullies!*" I screamed after them. "Stinking ugly bullies."

Olmstead tried to hush me up.

"I won't hush up," I cried. "They are bullies . . . and *cowards . . . and they ought to stay here and fight.*"

"You don't mean that," Olmstead said. "They're bullies for sure, but they'd kill us both and not give it a thought. Halvorsons think they own this valley." He helped steady me as I looked around in the gray light for my crutches. "You must have been scared," he said. "I hope you're not hurt."

"I'm not hurt and I wasn't scared, and you're as much of a bully as they are. Why didn't you stop them sooner?"

"I would have stopped them sooner, but I didn't think I could. There's only one of me, lots of them. And they're bigger, tougher, meaner. I didn't think they'd listen."

"*That's no excuse,*" I blubbered. "*No excuse at all.*"

He looked down at me, frowning. "For such a feisty little female, you are not realistic. Doesn't this attitude ever get you in trouble?"

"That's none of your business . . . none of your business at all." It hurt me that he had witnessed my helplessness, that he had seen them humiliate me, that he had heard what they'd said about me. It was this as much as anything that made me hate him. And I did hate him. I hated him as much as if he'd done those things himself. "I've got to get home," I said, my teeth chattering. "They'll be worried."

He offered me his hand. "My name's Oskar. Oskar Olmstead."

"Just don't t-touch me." If I once loosened my clenched jaws I'd start crying and I wouldn't be able to stop. I was numb with cold and my face burned with pain. "I've got to find my crutches and see to my pony. I've got to get home."

He brought me my crutches, found me my mittens, slapped the snow off my hat, and placed it firmly on my head. "I'm sorry about what happened. I'll see to the pony and sleigh."

"Leave me alone. Don't even t-talk t-to me. I'll do it myself. I hate you. You're one of them."

"I said I was sorry."

"You could have killed me. You could have killed my pony. If Katie and Charles had been with me you could have killed them. If anything happened to Princess it's all your fault," I wailed.

"My fault?" His voice deepened with indignation. "How is it my fault? I was out in the woods feeding stock. I heard the commotion and got here as fast as I could."

"I don't care. I hate you."

Oskar hunched his shoulders and looked down at his boots. "Have it your way then. I'm going to look after the horse."

I hobbled along behind him, aching in every limb.

Princess was on her feet, deep in a drift that filled the roadside ditch, held there by the traces of the overturned sleigh. Oskar freed her from the traces and urged her up out of the deep snow until she stood in the road, quivering all over, her nostrils flared to pink, her eyes ringed with the white ring that means fear in horses. She had cocked one hoof at an awkward angle, and I thought she must have broken her leg, and we'd have to shoot her the way they had to shoot the hunter in *Black Beauty*. They'd have to shoot me first. I told Oscar this, that they'd have to get past me if they wanted to put Princess down, and he gave such a sweet gentle smile that I began to suspect I might have been wrong about him.

"You don't have to worry," he said. "I'm sure she's okay."

"Nothing's broken?"

"I've checked her all over and there're no broken bones."

I pointed to the awkward position of her hoof. "What about that?"

He gave me her reins. "Here, you hold her. I check it again, just to be sure." He spoke gently to the frightened little pony, and she seemed to grow calmer at the touch of his hands. He knelt at her side, well out of the range of her hooves if she decided to kick, and he probed gently all around the pastern. "Nothing there," he said at last, standing up. "She may limp for a while, and she's going to be skittish, but that's only natural. Why don't you let me drive her and lead my own horse behind? You'll likely be a little skittish yourself, after what you've been through."

He was right. I was more than glad that he offered to drive, though at that time I would never have admitted it, for I had lost more than my dignity and the bucket of bricks in that incident with the Halvorson boys. When Oskar had righted the sleigh and hitched Princess to it, and as we were driving away, I felt as though I'd left something valuable behind—my courage.

I was shaking so badly that Oskar pulled the bear-

153

skin closer around me, careful not to touch me in doing so. "I think you ought to go back to the school to get warm," he said. "I don't like the way you're shaking. I've brought in young calves no bigger than you; shaking like this they sometimes go into shock and we lose them. The school's lots closer than the farm." Before I had given my answer he had turned the sleigh in that direction.

"Papa Joe will be worried. I should have been home by now."

"I'll ride up to the house, tell them what happened."

Suddenly I imagined the scene: Papa Joe in a tizzy, Ambrose cursing, Mama upset and flustered over the trouble I'd brought them. "I'd rather you didn't tell them the truth," I told Oskar. "I'll wait and tell them myself."

"I hate to think they might get away with what they did. You ought to talk to the sheriff." Oskar's lean face looked grim. "They could have hurt you."

"They did hurt me."

"They could have killed you, then."

"But they didn't." I couldn't tell Oskar my fears of being sent back to Missouri and going into an institution. I couldn't tell him I'd have to rely on Timothy to find a place that would take me in. I hated to admit that I was unwanted. I'd rather take on the whole gang of Halvorsons than do that.

Princess had not been injured as much as I'd feared. She started with a limp, pulling the light sleigh across the ice and snow, but the limp soon disappeared and she marched straight ahead with her head held high and her ears pricked forward as if listening for the bullies to come back. Oskar told me to talk to her to calm her. "She knows your voice and she trusts you."

154

On the ride to the school I was able to get a better look at Oskar, for the morning had grown much lighter and I was less emotional now that Princess and I were safe. He was younger than I'd thought at first, nineteen or twenty, of a slight build, with a face that was lean and intense. It was too dark to determine the color of his eyes, though I assumed they were blue because his hair was a shaggy dark blond and because his name was Olmstead. His ears stuck out like jug handles. He smelled of cows and hay, and I liked sitting next to him. I liked his warmth. I liked him. At the same time I hated him, too. He'd seen me as a fool.

He drove me right to the door. "I'll put Princess in the pony barn and find her some hay. Don't you worry about a thing. I'll be back this afternoon to see you safely home."

"Thank you."

"Are you still mad at me?" His voice sounded anxious.

"I don't know."

"I hope you aren't mad, because I am really sorry about what happened."

I should have forgiven him right away, but I was suffering from the cold and the kind of confusion that anger and fear can create, so I went on up the steps of the schoolhouse, opened the door, and let myself inside without having sorted out my feelings.

Inside the building, the room smelled like any classroom I'd ever known: wet woolen garments, floor wax, orange peel. Twenty blond heads bent over their desks. I spotted Katie in her new dress and Charles toward the back of the room, gazing into space. Neither of them noticed me at first. I felt cold and disheveled, as out of place as a storm-tossed bird that had just blown in. One little boy looked up from his book; his eyes went round and serious, and I was afraid he was going to laugh. I wanted to whirl around and dash out of the room. Since it's hard to dash anywhere on crutches, I stood my ground.

Katie looked up. "Gabriella?"

Charles was out of his seat, rushing toward me with outstretched arms. "Gabriella? Are you all right? Is something wrong? You look . . . different."

"I'm okay," I whispered. "Princess and I had a little accident, nothing important. But let's keep this a secret, all right?"

"I promise."

Then Katie was hugging me; and then she was introducing me to the teacher, who was looking down, taking my hand, being kind and gracious and pretty. "Old Mrs. English," as the children had called her, when talking about her at home, was not much older than I was. Her reddish brown hair swept up to a knot on her head, with tendrils of curls falling fetchingly across her forehead and the base of her neck. An expression of surprised delight seemed a natural aspect of her personality.

"You must be Gabriella," she said. "I've heard so much about you from Katie and Charles. I'm so glad you stopped in. I hope you'll stay awhile."

"I wouldn't mind."

I don't know what they thought about my bedraggled state, but nobody asked. Mrs. English found me a comfortable old captain's chair in front of the big iron stove in the back of the room, found me a footstool and a fluffy cushion, then excused herself so she could return to her teaching. "It's third grade reading. If they don't get it now I'm afraid they never will. Every minute counts."

"Don't mind me. I'm here to observe."

For the first hour or so I did not observe much.

The quiet room, the roaring fire in the stove, the four strong walls did much to ease the state of my nerves. Yet each time a child dropped a book, tipped back in his chair, squeaked chalk against the blackboard I started as if at a shot. I was glad that Oskar would drive home with me later, but would I ever find the courage to drive Princess down that road again? Would the Halvorsons always be waiting for me? I was sure they would carry a grudge. I would never again feel safe.

I looked up and caught two children pointing at me and laughing. Actually, they were pointing at my feet, laughing because they could not reach the floor. When they caught me looking at them, they hid behind their hands and glowered. Tante Eloise, ever fond of wise sayings, had liked to observe: "If you meet someone who needs a smile, give him one of yours." So I gave the pair a balmy grin, leaned back in my chair, and tried to relax. As cold and terrified as I had been out there in the forest, I could have put up with worse than two harmless children. Wind whistled in the chimney and rattled the windows that reached to the ceiling. The fire in the heater sent out a strong steady heat, thawing my frozen limbs. For a while at least I was safe.

Mrs. English woke me at lunchtime to ask me if I'd like a cup of soup. "It's only Campbell's, nothing like the good Bohemian cooking you're used to, but it's hot."

I followed her into the teacherage, where she showed me a sink with running water, electric lights that switched on and off, and an electric hot plate for cooking. "Compliments of the REA," she said. "Schools are first on their list. That's one of the perks of teaching. I've even got a radio. Still it gets lonely." She shuddered. "These long winter nights when the wind blows I almost go crazy. In the day there's the children, but then they go home and it's night again. At times I don't think I can stand it."

I climbed into a chair at the small dinette table that stood between the bed and the sink. "I know how it is."

She skipped over this. "I'm so glad you came to visit, Gabriella. I've sent note after note and none of the Shevalas have ever come. Katie is never a problem, but frankly I'm worried about Charles." She poured out the soup, put a box of Saltines on the table, got us each a spoon from the drawer. As she moved about she chattered. "Katie sits at the top of her class, but Charles is failing in everything."

"He's had a shock," I said. "He needs special understanding."

"I understand about his mother, how she said she'd come and then didn't. Frankly, Gabriella, I'm worried about him. He spends most of his school time daydreaming. He won't play with the other children, and now he's started stealing things. Little things, you know, pencils, crayons, scissors from the box, nothing big or important, but stealing is a symptom of unhappiness. Maybe if he had some extra attention. He's very fond of you, Gabriella . . ."

"I can give him extra attention. I could tutor him. I'm not stupid, you know. I do have a high school diploma. I would love to help him with his homework."

She spooned up her last dregs of soup. "You like those two children, don't you."

"I love them."

"They are lucky to have you, Gabriella."

We finished our soup, while the teacher rattled on and on, the way lonely people will, and I waited with dread for the day to end and dismissal. What if Oskar didn't show up? I kept my eye on the clock, and by the time four came around and the bell rang, the palms of my hands had started to sweat. The sky was dark with a gathering storm. Already flakes were starting to fly when I looked out the door and there was Princess hitched to the sleigh, ready to go. Oskar sat in the driving seat, reins in hand. He gave me a solemn wave.

I collected Charles's homework, collected both children, and said good-bye to Mrs. English, who begged me to come back. "You don't know how good it feels to have another adult to talk to," she said, tears in her eyes. "Sometimes I think I'll go crazy."

"I will, I promise."

The children and I climbed into the sleigh. Oskar had tied a lead rope from his own gray saddle horse to a ring on the sleigh, and the gray and my pony kept up a steady conversation, whinnying back and forth, which was more than I could say for Oskar and me. He didn't say more than two words as we drove through the forest and all the way up the long Shevala hill. When we got to the top and started down the long snowy lane to the house, he gave me the driving reins. "Tomorrow?" he said.

"Right here, eight o'clock."

He got out of the sleigh, untied his horse, swung into the saddle, and waited in the falling snow as I drove Princess toward home. Three times I turned around to see if he'd gone, but he hadn't. He was still there, a blurred figure on horseback, when I pulled the sleigh into the yard, and Papa Joe came running out to meet me. "Gabriella, little treasure, are you all right? We were so worried that something might have happened. Then that Olmstead boy said you'd stayed at the school to visit the teacher, but I never like to trust those Swedes."

"He was nice," Charles cried. "He drove us home."

Papa Joe skipped right over that. "Your preacher friend was here to see you. When you didn't come back he left, but he gave me this letter for you." Papa Joe handed me an envelope with my name written in ink on the front.

I wanted to open it then and there, but I couldn't, not with Papa Joe standing there in his shirtsleeves looking expectant. I wanted to read it in private, where I could savor every word, read it over and over, commit it to memory. I stuffed the letter into the pocket of my skirt, and Papa Joe led Princess down to the barn.

First, I had to help Mama put the supper on the table, and then we had to eat, and then there were the dishes to wash—at last I'd learned how!—and then I spent an hour with Charles on his homework. It was after nine-thirty before I was able to stagger up the stairs, exhausted, excited, to set the lantern bright on my bureau, and take the letter from my pocket.

As I opened it, carefully, I wished with all my heart that he could have been there in person. I could tell him about the Halvorson boys and how they'd humiliated me. I imagined how he'd fold me in his arms, how he'd whisper that I needn't be afraid, that he loved me, and that nothing else mattered but just us two, and that we'd be together, forever. Such was my dream.

I climbed up onto the bed, to settle myself in the depths of the goosedown comforter, and Goblin settled down with me, humming and purring, as I unfolded the letter and started to read.

# 15

My dearest Gabriella,

So sorry I missed you. I am going away but
will be back in late spring. Perhaps we can get
together then. I trust life is going better for
you, no more talk of institutions.

As always,
Tim

That was it? That was all? I turned the letter over,
as if he might have put his deeper feelings on the
back, but the back was blank. I opened the envelope
and peered inside, but it was empty. Goblin shoved
his big head against the letter; I pushed him away.
He shoved his head against the hand that pushed
him; I tossed him on the floor. With a loud meow,

161

he jumped back onto the bed. He pranced up and down the bedclothes, his tail in the air, as if trying to lift my spirits with his clowning, but I was not amused. I'd just been through one of the worst days of all the worst days in my life. I wanted sympathy, human sympathy. I wanted to pour out my story to someone who cared. From the tone of his letter, it was obvious that Timothy did not. I'd been an idiot to think otherwise.

Next morning I got up as usual, dressed in the flickering light, stomped crossly downstairs, burned the eggs, burned the bacon, burned the toast, and didn't care that I'd burned them. If I was treated unfairly by the world, then the world had better look out. Just as always, Papa Joe had Princess ready with the sleigh, and when the children tumbled out of the house with their books and wraps and lunchboxes, I touched the reins to the pony's back, starting her off at a brisk trot.

As promised, Oskar was there to meet me. He sat on the big gray horse and grinned foolishly when I ignored his greeting. "You're not still mad at me," he said, touching his hat as a sign of respect. "Are you?"

I clenched my jaws and urged Princess to pass him by. He was no better than the others. He was a fake, an oaf, and probably in cahoots with the Halvorsons. Papa Joe said he himself couldn't trust Swedes, and Olmstead was as Swedish as you could get.

"What's the matter?" Charles asked, anxiety rising higher in his voice. "Don't you like Oskar? I thought he was nice."

"He is nice, Charles. I'm just not in the mood to talk to him, that's all."

Katie came to my defense. "Gabriella doesn't have

to talk to him if she doesn't want to." To me she said, "*Why* don't you want to talk to Oskar? Did he insult you?" She waited a moment, while the pony's hooves kept a steady pace on the hardened snow, "Then, did he try to get fresh with you? Our mother has that problem a lot. She says you have to learn to ignore them when they try to get fresh, especially when you don't want them to."

"No, Katie, he didn't try . . ."

I was starting to feel ashamed of my rude behavior, when I heard the gray horse catching up to us, keeping pace with us, and then I saw Oskar's lean face looking at me, puzzled and somewhat amused, which only set me back into my anger. What right did he have to laugh at me? I slapped the reins harder against the pony's back, she stretched into a faster gait along the familiar route, but Oskar slapped his mount with his hat and tore away from us at a gallop.

The moment he was gone I wished I'd treated him better. I could be ambushed again, the children could be hurt, and I would have put us all in danger simply because of my whims. But we had come to the base of the hill and turned onto the road that led to the Bad Horse school when I caught sight of Oskar's dark outline riding well ahead of us, but obviously he hadn't deserted us. As much as I hated relying on him to protect us, I was relieved to know he was there.

The next morning I was afraid he hadn't come at all. However, we had only reached the base of the hill, and there he was on the big gray horse, his hat on his head like a distant beacon ever before us. It was the same every day. Since the morning I'd snubbed him he didn't bother to speak, and I was ashamed that I'd taken out my feelings of hurt and disappointment on him. Morning after morning when he appeared like clockwork, I realized that Oskar Olmstead was indeed a good person. I wished I had treated him better. Why is it we always learn these lessons too late? I was certain that Oskar would never speak to me again; I wouldn't have blamed him.

After the first day that I'd spent at the school, the lonely Mrs. English seemed almost desperate to get me to pass more time there. I had caught up on the work that Mama Shevala assigned me: mending, darning, hemming new tea towels, and all the basic cleaning. In addition she'd taught me to knit and crochet, skills I never thought I'd be able to learn— but I did. (I was knitting myself a sweater out of odd balls of yarn left over from past projects. It would be a strange sweater, kelly green, maroon, snowball white, and royal purple, but I didn't care. What did it matter how I looked? At least it would be good and warm.)

"If you are finished with your work, Gabriella," Mama told me as we were cleaning the table after supper one night, "I don't know why you shouldn't be able to stay over at the school. If you're sure the teacher doesn't mind."

"She keeps asking me to stay. She wants me to help her with the little ones, help them with their spelling words, hear them read. They're putting on a play, and she says she would like some help making costumes."

Mama Shevala took a bucket from the stove and poured hot water into the dishpan sitting in the sink. I would wash the dishes, she would dry. I climbed up onto the chair and started in. Since I'd last heard from Timothy I'd become more concerned than ever that the Shevalas not send me away and was always in a dither, looking for more work that I could do. Still, I'd begun to look forward to spending more time at the school. Housework, sewing, driving the children to and fro were not enough to keep my spirits from flagging. There ought to be more to life than work.

And that was how I got started at the Bad Horse school. At first it was as hurtful as I'd expected: children snickered, poked fun, called me names behind my back. Whoever says that children are basically kind has never known children. They are not kind; they are savages, as brutal and cruel as our cave-dwelling ancestors. The more secure they are within themselves, the more they love to torture anyone who is radically different. I knew this before I ever started to take part in the children's activities, and somehow I had to help them overcome their difficulties before I could ever hope to help them with their studies.

It embarrassed Katie and Charles so to hear the things the children said, and Charles was constantly in tears, begging me to find something else to do each day. "If they keep calling you names," he said, "I'll have to beat them up, and most of them are bigger than me."

"Face it, kiddo," said his sister, "everybody's bigger than you."

I didn't point out that they were also bigger than I was. I would have to rely on what I'd learned of human nature. When I told Mrs. English my plan she was against it. "If it doesn't work they'll massacre you."

I thought of Eileen Prestrude back at the academy, and Alice, and the Sylvia Plus misadventure. "I've been massacred before, and I imagine I will be massacred again before my life's over."

"This must be very important to you, then, to put yourself at such risk."

"I'm praying for a miracle."

What Mrs. English couldn't know was that the risk involved more than what I would suffer in front of the children, but also Oskar wouldn't know about my change in schedule and I'd have to ride back through the forest without his protection. He'd been so faithful all this time that I'd gradually lost my fear of the Halvorsons.

That same morning, when the bell had been rung and the children had gone through their morning exercises, pledging allegiance, singing two verses and two choruses of "America the Beautiful," I told their teacher I was ready for the first part of my plan. "Lift me up," I told her, "and stand me on the table."

She scrunched up her face and looked very disapproving.

"Please. It's the only way."

She did as I asked, standing me on the rectangular table between the rows of desks and the blackboard that covered the front wall of the classroom. She handed up my crutches and I stood there in my charity dress, my falling down socks, and my ill-fitting oxfords with the crumpled-up paper stuck in the toes.

The room fell instantly silent. All eight grades stared at me in astonishment, the lower grades seated closer to the stove, the middle grades getting out their spelling books, the four seventh and eighth grade boys sullen in the corner; they looked as though they couldn't believe what they saw. One of the little ones made a silly noise, and someone shushed him.

"You all know me," I began. "I work for the Shevalas . . ." My voice was so tense it rose higher and higher with every word. My face was on fire. "My name is Gabriella, and I would like to spend some time on these snowy days . . ." I stopped midphrase. Anson Anderson, in the eighth grade corner, had gotten out his spitwad collection and was readying his rubber band. In front of Anson, Karl Haagblom was folding paper planes. ". . . some time on these snowy days," I continued, "to help you sew costumes for your play. And Mrs. English needs some help hearing lessons . . ." Even before the first catcall I knew I should not have attempted this. My plan would never work. I'd been stupid to try it. Mrs. English was right: I was about to be fried.

I was looking around for the teacher to help me down, when the first airplane hit. And that did it. I would not have climbed down from that table if they'd brought in a team and tried to drag me down.

The teacher was trying to help. *"Please,"* she shouted, *"students.* Boys and girls, I'm ashamed of you." She lifted her arms to help me down, but I had other plans. I stood as tall as I could and started once again to speak.

By this time the room was in a shambles. No one was listening to anything I said. I was showered with spitwads. Paper planes dive-bombed from every side. Still, I kept talking, hoping wildly that the attacks would stop. ". . . you know you are behaving very badly," I said, and when a plane with a bobby pin centered in the prow struck me in the head, just above my eye, I was tempted to sling the plane back, but didn't. "The reason you are behaving as badly as you are is because you haven't taken time to get to know me. You see me as a dwarf, a funny-looking person, and that scares you because maybe you're funny-looking, too. Or you think you're funny-looking, or you're afraid someday people will discover that you're funny-looking, and it's easier to laugh at me. That way the pressure's off you."

I hadn't raised my voice at all. I'd trusted they'd

be so curious about what I had to say that they'd quiet down to listen. And that was what happened. The spitwads still flew, paper planes still blizzarded around the room, but the students were growing quieter, except for the occasional hoot, catcall, and whistle.

"Now, ladies and gentlemen, I am going to give you the chance of a lifetime. I'm going to let you ask me any question, any question at all . . . how it feels to be like me. I don't care how embarrassing it is."

There was a loud rude noise from the back of the room, but I'd caught their attention. They were listening. "There's only one condition. I'll answer any question you want to ask me today, and after today I won't answer any. So get your questions ready. This is your first and last chance."

I heard a lot of nervous giggles, mostly from the little kids. I had tried to avoid looking at Charles and Katie, but now I dared to glance about the room, looking for them. I spotted little Charles standing beside the teacher, pressing as close as he could get. She had her arm around him, and I could see how worried he'd been. The last thing I'd ever wanted to do was to make him afraid. I was stricken at the thought of how selfish I'd been. But then I saw Katie. She caught my eye and raised her hand. "I want to ask a question, Gabriella."

"Go ahead."

"How do you feel when people make fun of you and laugh at you?"

"It hurts like crazy."

The silence that followed could have been cut with a knife.

After that, the rest was easy. Oh, not easy, baring your weaknesses is never easy, but it's better than making a secret of them. People mistrust secrets, and when they're mistrustful they're apt to turn mean. I'd had all the meannesses I could put up with, yet if I didn't want to be a hermit I would have to get along. It was worth the risk.

The questions were embarrassing; some of them I couldn't answer because I didn't know the answer: "Do people like you ever have babies? Do you ever fall in love? What kind of man would want to marry a person like you? Don't you wish you were normal? Do you think God is punishing you for something bad that you did? Is that why he made you so little? Could a doctor ever make you grow?"

I answered as well as I could.

By the time the teacher went to ring the recess bell I was exhausted. My face was wet with sweat.

Mrs. English had nothing to say when she helped me climb down, and I was afraid I'd offended her with my outrageous performance, but it was something I'd had to do; I tried to explain this to her, but she wouldn't let me. "What you did this morning took real courage, Gabriella. I'm not sure I could have done it. I was watching the children's faces, and I saw them turn from a sort of nasty brutishness to respect. They're going to love you, Gabriella. When you have that you can teach them anything you want."

"I'm going to teach them Shakespeare."

Her mouth dropped open. "Shakespeare?"

"Yes. Why not?"

"Well . . . why not, indeed?"

"Most of them won't go much farther than the eighth grade. They'll start to work on the family farm, and after that they won't have a chance to read Shakespeare. I'd hate to have them miss out."

The rest of the day went smooth as silk. I set to work helping the older girls cut out costumes for the play they were planning to do—*Seven Keys to Baldpate*, a long way from Shakespeare. I helped the younger children with their spelling and arithmetic, heard their reading, discussed geography with the older students, showing them where I'd come from, and described my life as I'd lived it in St. Louis, Missouri. By the end of the hour I had them laughing—laughing with me. And that was fun.

Not every day thereafter went as smoothly. The students were still a long way from Shakespeare. With Mrs. English teaching one half of the class, and with me teaching the other half, we managed to get through the basics and still have time to do the play they'd worked so hard to get perfect. We got through the regular classes in history, arithmetic, spelling, penmanship, and geography in the morning, taking the afternoon off for rehearsals. Everyone in the school had a part—though it meant we'd had to write in some parts to give the littlest their moments on stage. We had asked some of the fathers to build the stage and set up the heavy red curtain. The mothers were bringing potluck for after. *Seven Keys to Baldpate* had sparked a community awareness in culture. I was as excited as anyone.

All my waking hours were devoted to work. I didn't have to think about my brown-eyed young man while I was working as a chore girl. My disappointment didn't surface when I buried it under my interests at the Bad Horse School. The day before the play was to open, we all got a shock that was to put my aching heart deeper into hiding.

It was a Friday afternoon, nearing the end of February, and already we imagined we could detect the scent of spring in the air. It was four-thirty and still daylight. Princess was enjoying the change to warmer weather by stretching to her fastest trot and holding to it through the slushy snow. I tried not to think of Timothy and all the dreams I'd had, but it was difficult; the air was rich and sensuous after all the bitterness we had endured. Breathing in such heady air put me in mind of romance. Having known the real thing, I was no longer interested in reading about Rowena LeSage. But what could I do?

"I can't wait for Sunday night," Katie said. "Can you?"

"Pretend we're going to go to the dentist," said Charles. "That makes the time go faster."

"We're so proud of you, Gabriella," Katie announced, straight out of nowhere. She was still wearing her fright wig and makeup, because she was so excited after rehearsal she hadn't wanted to take them off. I'd never seen her so wound-up and happy.

"Me?" I asked, astonished. "Why are you proud of me? Mrs. English arranged for the play. I had nothing to do with it."

"We're proud of you because all the kids like you," said Charles. He threw his arms around me and nearly knocked my hat off. "You're the most popular person in school, and that makes us popular, too."

Of course this was music to my unaccustomed ears. "I wouldn't have dared to go inside if it hadn't been for you two."

"We're all three wonderful," said Katie, with a wicked gleam. She looked ghoulish with a wart in the middle of her forehead, green skin, and vile lipstick. She cackled in witchy fashion and made us laugh, until she started to sing, and Charles and I joined her, singing a crazy song we three had made up traveling to and from the school. Even the pony got caught up in the fun and wanted to run when we'd reached the top of the hill. Because of the slush on top of the iced-over lane, I had to hold her to a walk. She tossed her head and whinnied, while the children sang, and I noticed what I should have noticed before. Car tracks. They went down the lane toward the house. *Timothy.* My thoughts went wild. *He's come back.*

A green car stood in the drive in front of the hitch rail, a car with Washington plates. The children had become so silent that the only sound was the *clip-clip clop* of hooves on the ice. We had scarcely come into the yard when the door of the farmhouse flew open and a large woman with red hair and a raccoon jacket came slamming down the stairs. "Katie!" she cried, running toward us. "Charles!"

"Mother . . . ?"

She didn't so much as acknowledge my presence but shouted to a man standing just within the milk porch. "Stanley, we've got them. Jump in the car, let's go!"

By the time Papa Joe came running out, the man was inside the automobile, starting the engine, spinning the wheels, and spraying out mud as they left us, wide-eyed, behind. I hadn't even told the children good-bye. That's how fast they were gone.

# 16

Perversely, the weather turned nice. A chinook, Papa Joe called the warm wind that blew in from the east. It melted what remained of the snow, leaving islands of ice surrounded by patches of soft ugly mud across the landscape. Nobody mentioned the children, which made their absence even more painful for all of us. Even the old farm dog curled up on the step beside the outside door hid his face beneath his paws and would not look up except for his supper. Goblin ran through the house, calling with heartbreaking cries.

And not just the animals suffered. Papa Joe went into mourning and took to his bed all day Saturday and Sunday. Tasha spent the weekend in her room, "writing letters," she said, emerging now and then red-eyed and teary, to help me and Mama Shevala put a meal together out of whatever was handy. Mama told her she ought to go ahead and cry, that she'd feel better. "It's not right to keep your feelings bottled up," she said. "You just might explode." At which Tasha swung her black hair back over her shoulders, cut her eyes at me, and giggled. Even so her dark almond eyes were very shiny and she gave my shoulder a squeeze as I pushed my chair up to my place at the table. "You're the one I feel sorry for," she told me. "You'll never get to see your preacher again. Not if you go back to Missouri."

Later that evening, she and Mama helped me wash out my laundry and hang it on a folding wooden rack in front of the open oven so the clothes would dry. There was no question of our going to the schoolhouse to watch the play, for none of us felt much like laughing. Sunday evening at seven, just as the curtain would be going up for *Baldpate*, Mama took me aside and asked if I'd made any plans, and I had to say I had not.

"We would like to keep you on, Gabriella. But you know how it is with money so tight all over."

"I never expected to stay."

Goblin came up to my room to watch me pack, yet again. He sat in my open suitcase, uglier and less appealing than ever. He'd already grown to the size of a small terrier, with ratlike whiskers, large leathery ears, a ratty tail, and eyes that had graduated from kitten-blue to an aquamarine that sent shivers up my spine. Though I never once encouraged him, he refused to acknowledge my indifference and pressed himself upon me at every opportunity. He watched me now with utmost faith, waiting for me to come to my senses. It had become apparent that he planned to leave with me. This foolish admiration suddenly touched me so deeply that I caught him up in my arms, letting his long rodentlike tail drag to the floor, while his happiness soared in his chest like a winter wind caught in the chimney.

At about nine o'clock, Mama Shevala came up to say how very, very sorry she was that things hadn't worked out. She brought up my apron with the hearts and flowers and lace-edged pockets, washed and ironed and with a smidgen of starch in the lace to make the hearts stand out. "Papa Joe has found the cash to buy you your ticket back, and there's money for a taxi and one night in a cheap hotel, and we both expect that you will pay the money back just as soon as you can."

"You can trust me."

"You have an aunt in St. Louis, didn't you say?"

"Tante Eloise."

She looked blank.

"That's French," I explained.

"How nice for you. I wish I could speak French."

"Mmmmm."

"At least, Gabriella, you've learned to sew and keep house. You can cook without burning yourself, and you've learned how to get along with children. If it weren't for your condition you'd make some man a good wife. Perhaps you can find a position as a nanny. Nannies get to be almost like family, and that would be nice. I'd hate to think of you living out your life alone."

I was glad when she'd gone and Papa Joe had come up to help me with the heavy suitcase and cartons. The train left so early in the morning we had to have everything out on the milk porch, ready to load into the wagon before we left.

"It's not my idea that you go, little treasure." Papa Joe's face was drawn with misery. "And you can't blame Mama. She's a saint, a living saint, but she's had too much to put up with in life. She worries too much, always fussing that we can't afford this or that little luxury. And I try to tell her that you're not a luxury, that you're money in the bank, but she doesn't see it. She won't listen to me. She only has ears for that Ambrose. I've tried to tell her how we'll take you to the fair, and I've tried to tell her about the chariot, and how you'll fly by, dressed up like an angel with golden wings, and we'll make you a halo, and how the people will cheer . . ." His face wore a helpless look, and his arms hung loose at his sides. "What can I do?"

"It's all right, Papa Joe. I understand."

"You ought to go say good-bye to your pony. Ponies grieve. You might not know that, but ponies and horses can grieve themselves to death, just like people."

"I will." I reached for my crutches. "I'll go right now."

Goblin went with me, racing down the stairs, then whirling around and racing back up the stairs so he could come down with me at a slower pace.

In the parlor, Ambrose was sitting in what had been my chair in front of the glowing stove with his stockinged feet propped up on the woodbox. Mama and Tasha must have gone to their rooms. For once Ambrose looked deeply, genuinely pleased with his life. He was cleaning his fingernails with his hunting knife and gave me a smile that I did not return.

"I see," he said, quietly, slyly, as I swung by, "that my letter to Katherine got results."

"Letter? What letter?"

"Oh . . . the usual family letter. She is my sister, you know."

Something cold-blooded about his manner put me on guard.

"What did you say in your letter to your sister?"

"The truth." He discovered a flaw, some irregular point or corner on the nail of his little finger, and pared at it with his knife.

"It was about me, wasn't it?" I stood there, framed between crutches, as the light in the room grew dim and my thoughts surged. "What did you tell her, Ambrose? I need to know."

"Nothing much. I let her know what kind of person was looking after the precious kids that she deserted. She's a lousy mother and she knows it, but she's full of guilt. I know how to bring her around. I only did what I had to."

If looks could kill, Ambrose would have dropped like a rock to the floor. *"Tell me. What was in that letter?"*

"I told her that you were a freak."

*"You didn't."*

"It's true. You are a freak. Why pretend you're not? You ought to be in a circus."

*"You're wrong."*

He examined his nails for further imperfections, then buffed them lazily against one sleeve. "You could have fooled me."

If he'd struck me a hammer blow direct between the eyes he could not have hurt me more. With the cat running at my side, I staggered out of the room, through the kitchen to the porch, and out into the warm chinook night, reeling from his remarks. The moon was full, with a gauzy light that made the distant white mountains stand out against an inky sky. I would never see those mountains again, never see this same sky, never stand in this yard again. I would never drive the sleigh and pony again, or hear the rooster crow—or see Charles and Katie again.

Deafened as I was by my own self-pity, I hadn't noticed the farm dog's barking in the lane until a horse and rider appeared, a single black shadow that slipped in and out of patches of moonlight. *Tasha's lover*, I thought. *Why couldn't it be mine?* I called Shep to my side to quiet him. Goblin stood staunchly by my side, fearless as ever. Goblin didn't know I was a freak—or knowing, didn't care. He would stay by me no matter what. And I would have to leave him behind.

Horse and rider drew nearer, paused at the hitch rail, and the rider dismounted. It was not Nils Halvorson at all. It was Oskar. I watched as he tied his horse to the rail and then I called to him in a shaky voice. "Oskar? Over here."

"Gabriella? Miss Wheeler?"

Because of the beating my confidence had taken I was hardly able to speak, and it occurred to me that I would be leaving Oskar, too. Not that it mattered. What could he care about a freak? He had been kind to me, and I was grateful. I hated to have to be grateful for kindness.

"Gabriella? Is that you?"

As if I could have been somebody else. A cloud scudded across the moon and scudded away again, driven by a light warm breeze.

"Gabriella, it's me. Oskar."

"I know." I stood where I was. "What is it, Oskar? What do you want?"

"Are you all right?" He drew nearer. In the gauzy light I could see only his outline, not his face, and as he approached I sensed his concern . . . but was it real?

"Are you all right, Gabriella? You sound funny.

Has something happened? Where are Katie and Charles? When you didn't show up for the play everyone wondered. You aren't sick, are you? I left the play early and came looking for you. I thought maybe . . . well, you know, after last time . . ."

"I'm okay."

His voice turned brusque. "You've had us so worried. You should have let us know you weren't coming."

"How?"

"I don't know how . . . but you should have."

"I'm sorry."

"Sorry? Is that all? Mrs. English had something to tell you, something important. Here, she wrote it down in this letter to make it official. She's going away next week and she wants you to take over the school. She's worked it out with the school board. She says you can take over on a substitute basis for the rest of the year, and then it's permanent . . . if it all works out, if you want to do it."

I stood there a moment, taking this in. The warm wind pushed against my shoulders, and from the dark in the direction of the horse barn Princess whinnied; Oskar's horse answered.

"What's the matter, Gabriella? Aren't you happy? I thought you'd be happy. The students like you, their parents like you, and you'd have a job where you could make some money, not much maybe, but it would be better than here. These Shevalas are taking advantage of you, Gabriella. You're getting nowhere. I wanted you to be happy."

"I am happy."

"You sure don't sound like it."

I had heard of the *Perils of Pauline,* and had often fancied myself Pauline-like, tied to the rails as the train whistle blew and the locomotive came screaming down the tracks. Once again I'd been rescued. I was grateful, of course, but after what I'd been through I was not ecstatic. I'd been saved—but for what?

Oskar gave me the letter.

I thanked him.

"You'll do it, won't you?"

"Yes."

The soft chinook wind rubbed its warm silk against my neck and hands and face. It tugged at Oskar's forelock. He looked down at his boots. "Well, okay then . . ." he drawled. "That's all I've got to say."

"Thank you for coming all this way." Brittle and ungracious, but what else could I do? Ask him to come in? Have a chat with Ambrose? Witness my disgrace? I had too much pride for that.

"I'm glad you're all right," he said once again, lingering.

"Thank you." This to dismiss him. I wanted him to go.

"Good-bye."

"Good-bye."

If I wasn't ecstatic, Papa Joe was. "Our little woman, our treasure, our pet, think of it! A teacher! Now what have you got to say to that, Ambrose, you snake-belly son? Didn't I tell you she had brains? Didn't I?" For the first time since the children had gone his long face brightened, eyes snapped, and he waltzed around the room, flapping his arms, crowing. Ambrose glowered by the fire.

Mama Shevala came out of her room, still in her nightgown. She'd taken out her teeth and had done her hair up in curlers. "It's all very well . . . if you can do it, Gabriella. *If*, I say. I'm not at all sure that you can. What if the children won't mind you when their regular teacher is gone? What will you do then?" She puffed at a wisp that had come loose from its curler, pushed it back with her thumb, but the wisp popped up again as always. "You with your French and your hoity-toity ways," she said. "You might think you're better than poor country people, but I think you will find, Gabriella, that children are not impressed with French or hoity-toity—I don't care what you say. Children need a teacher with both feet on the ground. They need someone who's normal, Gabriella. Normal."

She drew herself up to her fullest height and fluttered, partridgelike, out of the room. "I'm going to bed, everyone. Good night."

I couldn't wait to leave. As soon as I could I asked Papa Joe if I could borrow the old farm wagon to move myself and my things to the school. There wasn't enough snow left for the sleigh. Papa Joe wouldn't hear of it. "Farm wagon? Teachers don't travel in wagons—they travel in style."

"I haven't got any style, Papa Joe. I need the wagon."

"Ah, but you do have style, little one. Wait until you see it, my treasure . . . my latest present for you. I wanted to save it, but I will have to give it to you now."

"Please, Papa Joe," I heard myself cry, "I haven't got time for any more presents."

"Ah, that's what you say, but wait until you see it. Oh, but you're going to be glad."

Miserable, unhappy, nearly numb from the battering I'd just been through, I followed him out of the house and toward the barn. The ground was muddy on the surface and frozen underneath, so that my crutch ends struck ice as bitter as my heart. Goblin dashed ahead, his tail whipping, his eyes like two coals. Shep, who'd lived longer and had seen more, took the commotion in stride and trotted beside us at an old dog's pace. Most likely the night had grown colder, but if this was so I didn't notice. Cold I could endure; myself I could not.

He led me to the hay barn, a large ramshackle structure of silvered wood, half standing, half listing, mocking in the moonlight. I waited as he opened the door, waited as he fished around in his overalls pockets for matches, waited as he lighted the lantern that hung from a hook in an overhead timber.

"There you have it, my treasure." His voice grew tight with pride. "I made it myself."

The chariot.

"What do you think?" he whispered.

I gazed at the hideous contraption. Lantern light shed an orange-peel glow across three hens perched head to tail on the two-wheeled cart; light glinted from the gilt-trimmed rail, it accented the grinning faces of two fat cherubs carved in high relief above each wheel, and it shone dully from the old brass cowbell Papa Joe had bolted to the front like an idiot's bell to warn pedestrians out of the way. The effect made me gasp.

"Isn't it something?"

"It's . . . me."

The cold that I hadn't felt before sank into my flesh and gripped my bones. In spite of Papa Joe's objections, I insisted that we lead Princess from her stall and hitch her to the chariot right away. Complaining that the night was dark, that it wasn't safe for travelers, that I would get lost, that the wolves would find me, that the boogeyman would pluck me up and stuff me in his pocket, Papa Joe finally agreed to load my belongings into the chariot. He pushed everything forward for better balance and helped me climb up to the top. The cat jumped in beside me, I loosened the pony's reins, and we were off. One door had opened as another slammed shut behind me: My life as a chore girl had ended.

# 17

I would like to state here that my life as a teacher at Bad Horse School was a heavenly experience. Compared to the life I had known as a youngster locked away in an attic, or as a misfit at a girls' school, or as a chore girl on a farm, this might have been so. Otherwise it was not. I would like to state that the children I was responsible for were always angels; that I found only adoration in their eyes, love in their hearts, kindness in their ways, or that I earned enough salary at my new occupation to provide myself with comforts: But these would be lies.

I did have privacy, though. Mrs. English left just as soon as she could, "to take advantage of the chinook," she claimed, departing with one of the Haagblom brothers, who was kind enough to give her a lift into town, where she would catch the Greyhound back to Minneapolis to be with her family. She left on a Tuesday after a full day's teaching. The moment I saw the pickup leave the schoolyard, I locked the schoolhouse doors, hurried back to the teacherage—my new home—locked those doors, took off my shoes, tossed my crutches aside, and bounced up and down on the bed. No one to hear me, no one to care. I turned up the radio that Mrs. English had left behind. ("You'll never survive without it," she'd said. "The loneliness will get to you. You'll be mad before spring.")

By five o'clock our chinook had ended, and already it had started to snow. Wind slammed against the windowless side of the building. When I went out to see to Princess, flakes were swirling thick and soft, piling up on nearly barren ground. I pumped water from the stable pump to fill the pony's drinking trough, cut open a new bale of hay from the supply in the hay shed, carried the hay into the pony barn, and pitched it into the pony's manger. I made sure her stall was clean, then brought in more fresh golden straw until it was up to her knees and would keep her warm. She breathed her velvet breath against my face, nickered in her quiet way. I never got over her gentle ways. It was almost as though she sensed my physical fragility. That quality I most hated in myself she accepted, respected. She had become my friend. We trusted each other.

The mailman came every morning, with nothing for me. Every Friday afternoon a neighboring rancher would stop to pick up my grocery order. At first I ordered wildly: bakery cakes, boxes of chocolate-covered cherries, whole canned hams, jars of olives, and cases of Nehi's orange pop. Every evening as I sat at the table, grading papers, making out lesson plans, and worrying over seat work that would keep my students busy, Goblin perched on top of the bookcase, watching in dismay as I turned into a butterball.

Not that he was much better. For him I ordered cans of tuna fish, cans of salmon; he caught fat gray mice, which lived in the barn and in the school, as well. For Goblin, Bad Horse School became a paradise. Except when I was teaching he never left my side. Along with Princess he'd become a close friend.

I wasn't so lucky with the children. I had thought and thought about Mama Shevala's prediction—that the children wouldn't mind me when the regular teacher was gone—and her prediction had made me so afraid that what she'd said soon came true. As wild animals will catch the scent of fear and then attack, my students did this, too. Not surprisingly the Halvorson youngsters were the worst. They hadn't broken out into full-fledged revolution, not yet, but they were rumbling. I wasn't sure how much longer I could hold them.

One afternoon, as class was dismissed, I saw a slight figure approaching on horseback. I gave the bell rope an extra tug when I saw him and waited until the last little boy had buckled his overshoes, the last little girl had found her lost mitten and her lunchbox, the last of the eighth graders had turned in his essay, before I looked up and acknowledged Oskar's presence. I didn't want him to guess how very glad I was to see him. It wouldn't do to seem overeager, but I had missed him.

"Howdy," he said, and touched his hat.

"Hello."

"How's it going?" He searched my face with calm gray eyes. "Kids behaving?"

"Oh, my, yes. They're angels." I'd almost forgotten his homely face, the jug ears. When he took off his hat, his mop of darkish blond hair was longer, shaggier, more unruly than ever. He gave me a lopsided grin. "I've been thinking about you. I've been wanting to drop by, but I know how you feel about people interfering . . ." His grin stretched wider. "I didn't want to get you mad at me again."

It felt good to laugh again with someone my age. "May I fix you some coffee?"

He seemed genuinely pleased. "I'd like that, Miss Wheeler. I'd like that an awful lot."

It was the first time in my life that I'd been able to entertain, and I realized suddenly that I didn't have any coffee. I explained this to Oskar. "All I've got is Nehi's orange."

"That's even nicer," he said. "I never did like coffee. I only drink it to be polite. I hate the taste."

I opened two bottles of pop, took down two glasses from the counter, placed them on the table. "How about a slice of bakery cake?"

"No, thanks. The pop'll do fine."

We sipped at the sweet orange-flavored pop. Oskar got a stencil-thin orange mustache that tilted upward in a grin. I knew I had one, too, but I wouldn't wipe it off. It made me feel racy, daring.

"I dropped by," he said, "to give you a letter."

"Oh, my . . ." I was flirting a little, rolling my eyes, laughing too quickly at every little thing. "Is this letter anything like the last letter you brought me? You know you ought to get a paycheck for delivering mail." I laughed and he laughed because I did, not because I'd said anything really funny.

"I don't know who it's from." He reached into his back pocket and pulled out a long white envelope, slightly the worse for its travels. "I delivered a load of hay up to Papa Joe's, and they said you had this letter waiting there, and if I was ever up this way would I deliver it? I said I would."

*Timothy.*

All the blood in my body raced straight to my head. I forgot I'd been flirting with Oskar. I forgot Oskar.

The letter was thick. I tore off the tiniest little strip of envelope, not wanting to tear a single precious word that was written inside. And all this while Oskar was talking and talking, and I wasn't listening. Only later would I think back, desperate to remember what he'd said: He was giving me a warning.

He was telling me that Tasha had disappeared from the farm, and everyone believed that she had run away with Nils Halvorson, and now Ambrose was on a rampage. He and Papa Joe had come to blows at last, and, strange as it seemed, Mama had thrown Ambrose out. Nobody knew where Ambrose had gone, but it was certain that he was out looking for Nils and Tasha. "I'm afraid for you," Oskar said. "I'm afraid Ambrose might show up here."

"Mmmmm . . ." I said, lost in my letter. "That's nice."

"I don't think you know what you're saying, Gabriella. Ambrose is out of his mind. He could hurt someone."

"Mmmm . . . um hmmm." Tim's letter went on and on about the Lord, about all He had done for Tim, all that Tim had done for Him, and how much we all had to be thankful for. I was poring over the fine curved script searching for specific mention of me. And found it. Eureka!

"Promise you'll keep your doors locked, will you, Gabriella?"

"My letter's from a wonderful friend," I said,

wanting to share my secret, but not the whole secret. "He says he's coming to see me soon. He has a proposal for me, that's what he says."

"A friend?" Oskar grew quiet.

"A young man of my acquaintance."

"I see. Is he a . . . special friend?"

"Oh, very special."

I had already put Oskar so completely out of my head that I hardly noticed when he'd gone, and it wasn't until late that night when the wind started up from the north, when the old building creaked and groaned and when Princess whinnied loudly from her stall that I thought of what Oskar had been trying to tell me, that my life was in jeopardy. An exaggeration, surely.

Homework corrected, quizzes made out and already written up on the blackboard to be ready for morning, lesson plans written neatly in the plan book, I was sitting up late rereading my wonderful, wonderful letter from Timothy; the heating stove snapped and popped with a rowdy little fire. The wood was full of sap, and I knew just how it felt, for I was full of it, too. How wrong I'd been to give up my dream. How wrong I'd been to doubt my brown-eyed young man. How wrong I had been to doubt *love*. Feet to the fire, I leaned back in my chair and went back over the "good parts" again:

> . . . may have seemed as though I'd forgotten you, my dearest friend, but such was never the case, believe me. You are ever in my prayers. Your gentle face and loving ways have been engraved upon my heart. You are the first friend I shall call upon when I return to Montana. I have a favor to ask of you—and I have a proposal for you. This could be very soon, as soon

as the weather turns warm. I am entered into a new phase of ministry, dear one, and I will be at the riverside to conduct a very special service of prayer and healing . . . keep me safe in your heart, little one, and I shall keep you safe in mine. Remember, this above all, you are loved . . .

Knowing this, believing this, I was ready for anything.

In a vague and dreamy state, I heated water in buckets on top of the heating stove, exchanged the harsh glare of electric light for the soft glow of candles, and when the water was warm I took a long leisurely bath in a laundry tub. Mrs. English had neglected to take some of her personal things in her flight from the school, and among them I'd found a jar of bubble bath that featured a long-legged seductress silhouetted on the front, with breasts like the points of Cupid's arrows, yet she was no more glamorous than I, for I was loved. Loved. No more Rowena LeSage. This love didn't come from a book. It was real.

As I sat deep in bubbles, steam rising around me, the fire crackling merrily to keep the room warm, Goblin sat on a kitchen chair I had drawn up beside the galvanized tub. He watched in amazement as I soaped my neck and elbows; he snaked out a large gray paw and swatted at the bubbles, astonished when they burst at his touch. His bluish-green eyes grew round, and he swatted again and again, reaching out farther each time, until he slipped and fell in. Up to his chin in bubbles and water, he gave me a long disgusted look, yelped, and hauled himself out, trailing water across the floor as he fled to hide under the bed.

I was afraid he'd catch cold, so I climbed out, dried off on a towel I had hung over the back of the chair, facing the heater, then climbed under the bed to coax Goblin out. Though it was for his own good, he refused to come out, but crawled farther and farther beneath the bed, making me go under all the way to scramble among the dust bunnies to get him. I wrapped him in a warm towel of his own, pulled on one of the soft flannel robes Mama Shevala had made me, and sat down with him by the fire.

It was then I thought I heard someone call my name.

I held the purring cat . . . listened. *Thump*.

Outside in the constant storm, something rattled and bumped. I thought I heard something heavy clumping back and forth on the roof. But then I heard my name again, thin and distant, lost in the keening of the wind. By now I was scared. I thought of what Oskar had told me and wished I'd listened better.

Something heavy slammed into the door. It sounded a lot like an axe. Goblin jumped down, and I got to my feet, waited, ears strained. I heard the loud sound of banging. Whatever had been trouncing about on the roof had stopped and was banging at the door. I picked up a stout stick of stove wood, tied my sash securely at my waist to keep the robe shut, and unlocked the door that led into the schoolroom. How cruel it would be if I were killed before spring. After such a long winter, not to see the summer sun.

*"Gabriella?"*

This time I heard it, each syllable distinct. I pulled my robe closer against the cold and against my own fear, and I heard it again: a girl's voice, lilting, scared. It could have been a trick . . . or it could have been someone in trouble. I couldn't leave her out there in the open blizzard.

"Who is it?" I put my ear to the door and listened.

*"Gabriella, let me in."*

"Who's out there?"

There came a long pause, then: *"Gabriella, it's me . . . Tasha."*

Quickly I unbolted the door, let her creep in, a small pathetic creature, wrapped in her long black cloak and hood, and I bolted the doors again. "Come on," I urged her, "come back to the teacherage, get yourself warm. You must be frozen."

Inside my private quarters, I found the light switch and turned on the lights. Tasha gasped and let out a tiny scream, so I doused the light but left the candles burning. I couldn't help but comment on her appearance. This person I had always envied looked frightened and disheveled. Her face was drawn and white beneath the dark hood, her long black hair tangled in knots and rimed with frost. "What's happened to you, Tasha? You look half-frozen."

"It's Ambrose, he found out about us." She settled herself on the very edge of the bed to tell me the story. "He found out about me and Nils. He's looking for me now . . . he says he'll kill me."

"He hates Nils that much?"

"He hates the Halvorsons that much. He feels humiliated, inferior. He hates everybody now, you, me, Papa Joe . . . there isn't anyone who's safe, but mostly he wants to hurt me. Me and Nils." She glanced wildly about the tiny room. "You haven't seen him, have you? He isn't here?"

I assured her he was not. "Oskar came by and told me that you and Nils had already run away. I thought you two would be married by now."

"I've been trying to get away," she said, on

the verge of tears. "I've been hiding in sheds and barns . . ." She made a face. "Oh . . . you wouldn't believe the things I've been through. Nils couldn't come to the farm because Ambrose had a gun and nobody knew where he was."

"Tasha, I'm so sorry."

"Can I stay here until morning? Nils said he'd come here to pick me up, then we're taking the train and going to California." Her voice became gentler, softer, womanly. "We're going to live in California, think of it. We're going to sleep together always. We'll have our babies in California."

"California will be wonderful, after all you've been through." I said this to calm her, for she sat perched on the edge of the bed, trembling like a storm-tossed bird, her hands clenched in her lap. "So much sunshine," I said, "so many flowers, and you can open your kitchen window and pick oranges for breakfast, so I've been told."

The wind roared like a beast trapped in the chimney. Old boards creaked and sang. Again I heard the thumping and bumping overhead, then forgot it as a burning ember shot out through the door of the roaring stove. It was hissing and spitting in the snow that Tasha had tracked on the floor. I caught it up in the fire shovel, put it back inside the stove, and closed the iron door to conserve heat. In the next moment I heard a great slide of snow slip like an avalanche from the schoolhouse roof, and in that moment I knew—*knew*—that this was a sign: Winter had ended.

Tasha fell asleep in the big chair by the fire. I threw a blanket over her to keep her warm, then stayed awake myself, startled and anxious over every little sound. Toward morning the wind died down and I heard coyotes yapping in the hills. From far away a farm dog answered; it could have been Shep. How worried Papa Joe and Mama must be about Tasha. Mama would be grieving for her difficult son, for I knew that she loved him. I thought of my own mother and of how she had grieved because of my father: how difficult and wearying families can be, yet how sad it is to have none.

If Ambrose was still waiting outside in the dark he kept his presence secret. I fell asleep as the sun was beginning to peek in through the window; when I awoke, Tasha had gone.

# 18

I shall always be grateful that it was one of the Hagen boys who found him, and not a Halvorson. Lee Hagen, one of the nicer, quieter, members of my sixth grade class, came running inside with the news. He had been playing tag with six other boys and had run around to the windowless side of the school-house, the side most battered by winds, and he had hidden in the crevass between the wall of the school-house and the big drift of snow left over from winter. The drift still reached nearly to the roof, though everywhere else the snow had melted away to crisp green grass.

It was a sunny day, mild and scented with cat-kins. Princess was grazing in the field, Goblin sitting on a fencepost enjoying the sun. It was almost *time,*

I had been telling myself for a week now. He'll be here in the spring . . . and it was spring. I would see him *soon*. I'd just left my desk and gone to the cloakroom to pull the bell rope to end recess, when Lee came running in.

"*Miss Wheeler . . . Miss Wheeler . . .*" He was all out of breath. "There's something out there buried in the drift . . . and it looks like a black bear or something. It's scary, Miss Wheeler. Come see!"

"In the drift? Is it living or dead?" I had not the slightest desire to tackle a black bear, living or dead, but if given my choice I'd prefer that it be dead. I let go of the bell rope and tucked my crutches under my arms. "Take me to it."

He was sitting upright. The snow had only partially melted, exposing the straight black hair. By this time the children had gathered around and I motioned for them to stay back; I knew by this time what we had found. I climbed partway up the drift and brushed the snow away from the face and stared into dark taxidermy eyes that stared back at me. I remembered all too well that sudden slide of snow and my own conviction that a hard cold season had ended. Ambrose had been up on the roof and had fallen to his death.

Later, when the sheriff arrived with the coroner, and they shoveled the body out to carry Ambrose away, I couldn't stop myself from crying. I'd hated him. He'd made my life hell with his undeviating cruelty, yet I felt sorry for him, too. He was the other side of me: If I hadn't found love I would have been no different from Ambrose, frozen with resentment and rage, dead to the world, dead inside.

I spent the rest of the day in the teacherage, sitting in the big chair by the window, crying and crying.

Oskar dropped by that evening and found me there. He did his best to comfort me. "I know how you feel, Gabriella. You're so forgiving. You have such a tender heart." He put his arm around my shoulders. He held me gently as if I might break. "Gabriella," he whispered in my ear, "I think you ought to hear the whole story."

I looked up at him, my face streaming. "You mean *why* he was up on the roof?"

"That's what I mean."

He told me then how the sheriff had climbed up the outside ladder to the chimney. "You know what he found up there? Gas-soaked rags, that's what. And there was a gas can buried with him in the snow."

"He was setting the schoolhouse on fire."

"Looks that way."

"I could have done that. It could have been me frozen in the snow." I thought of his glassy staring eyes, how they could have been my eyes frozen with hate.

Oskar protested. "You're the gentlest person I know."

I didn't tell him then, though I could have, how I would have burned the academy to the ground if I'd had the strength. I thought of all those girls, of how I'd wanted to be one of them, how they wouldn't have me—yes, I would have gladly burned them to the ground and danced around in their ashes. "You don't know me," I bawled, "what a terrible person I am."

And then Oskar went back to trying to comfort me again, which is not such an unpleasant way to spend a warm evening in early spring. By the time Oskar discovered that he'd stayed with me way past milking time and that he had to get home to see to the cows, we'd gotten to know each other in ways we'd never even thought of before.

Three days after Ambrose's death, Katherine came back for the funeral and brought the children. I had gone to the farmhouse to be with Mama and Papa Joe. In spite of our differences, I cared for them and knew they would want me there. No sooner had the boyfriend's car rolled into the yard than the car door flew open, and Katie and Charles were running toward me, arms outflung. They hugged me around the neck and I did the same, though both had grown so much taller I could hardly reach their cheeks to kiss them. Charles looked thin and had dark circles under his eyes. Katie's hair had been cut as short as her brother's; she looked gaunt and unhappy.

Charles was crying: "Gabriella, we've missed you. You can't even know how much we've missed you."

"Mother says we can stay here forever if we want," Katie whispered. "Even if you aren't living here anymore, we want to stay so we can see you and we'll have good times like we always did before."

"We will," I promised, holding her close. "We'll have good times, believe me."

Mama had become more gracious with grief. She asked about my work and how I liked it. "I've heard very good things about you," she said. "Some people say you're the very best teacher they've had up at Bad Horse."

I thanked her kindly. "Next year I'll do better."

Papa Joe had taken his son's death hard. The doctor who had cared for me during my long illness was there to tend to Papa Joe. "There's been so much anger," he told me when he and I were alone. "Papa Joe is going downhill. He's always been a little . . . well, a little off . . . but now he may never be right in the head. He can't forgive himself for all the bad feelings between himself and the boy. He can't face reality at all."

When I went into the bedroom to see him, Papa Joe looked pale and old. "Little treasure," he said, when he opened his eyes and saw me there at his bedside. "Do you know what has happened? No one will tell me the truth, they keep telling me lies. I trust you, little treasure. You're not like the others. I know you will tell me the truth."

Because it was Papa Joe, my old friend, I was caught off guard and taken in. "It's Ambrose," I began, ". . . there was an accident."

He looked at me a long, long moment, thinking this over. "No," he said at last. "That's not true. You're no better than the others." He turned his face to the bedroom wall as if to go to sleep, but his eyes were still open when I excused myself and left the room; he could not get up to go into town to the church for the funeral. I went in to say good-bye before I was to leave, and he had not moved. I stood by the side of the bed, looking across at him. If only I had something to give him, for he had given me so much.

"Papa Joe, you are loved," I told him.

When he made no response, I said it again: "You are loved."

I had no way of knowing if he heard me, or if what I said made the slightest difference, for he made no movement, made no sound. The next time I saw him, weeks later, the first of June, he seemed to have no memory of anything that took place during this time of grief. He never again mentioned Tasha, or Ambrose, or even Katherine, although her children had returned to make their home at the farm.

I did not go back to the farm after the funeral that

day. Time was fleeting; I had lessons to prepare for my students and I had to prepare for Timothy's arrival. The weather had grown steadily warmer. Snow melt had already swollen the swift-running streams, and it wouldn't be long before he would be here for those special services he would hold beside the river. Before that time came I wanted to be healthy, whole, and strong. I wanted to be ready.

I'd had yet another letter:

Most loving friend,

The time is nearly here. I have prayed much and long about what I am about to ask you to do. I hope you will not be upset, dear friend, for your feelings are always uppermost in my mind. You are so very dear to me, Gabriella. Keep your innocent goodness always, promise me that. Since that very first time, when we met on the train—remember?—your well-being has been my first concern. Hold this in your heart when I ask you my question, will you?

Until such time, know that you are loved.

Yours in Him,
Timothy

By this time I knew what my answer would be.

If the winter of my life had been long and desperate, this new season brought a happiness I'd only dreamed of. School let out in June and I was almost sorry to see my students go. All except my eighth graders would be back again next fall, and I had resolved to become a better teacher by then. I planned a summertime of reading and studying that would make me familiar with all the textbooks so that I wouldn't have to struggle just to keep a jump ahead.

For entertainment I'd spent some of my salary to

buy myself an electric sewing machine, and had spent a day in town shopping for patterns to modify to fit me and Mama Shevala had agreed to help me choose fabrics from the Montgomery Ward's catalog. I planned my wardrobe with as much excitement as if I'd been a beauty queen. Knowing I was loved had made me feel lovable; I wanted to be worthy of that love. I wanted him to be proud of me.

And then there were the children. Some days they stayed at the teacherage and we would spend happy hours walking through the fields, or riding Princess, or driving the silly-looking chariot about the countryside. As he grew stronger, Papa Joe took us all the places he'd promised: We went up Kelly Hill, where we ran into bears; we went fishing in Gold Creek, where Charles fell in and nearly drowned (but didn't!); we went swimming in the Whitefish River, and there was a forest fire (but we didn't burn up!).

Every day I did exercises to strengthen my legs, and just as the doctor in St. Louis had predicted they did grow stronger. I had given up my diet of bakery cakes and Nehi orange pop in exchange for chicken and rabbit casseroles, which I constructed on my hot plate; I ate fresh vegetables as they came in, drank cold milk, and thought only pure thoughts. I wanted to be ready for *him*.

As my legs grew stronger, strong enough to hold me upright without crutches, I found that I *had* grown taller. I had grown one whole inch taller! I'd been keeping my own measure, marking my advance against the doorframe to my room. On the day that I realized I had grown that full inch, Timothy came striding up and knocked at the open door. He stood there in the sunshine, in his boiled white shirt, his handsome jacket draped casually over one shoulder because of the warmth of the afternoon. He looked a little older than I remembered, and somewhat fatter—but then I'd grown used to skinny Oskar. He looked down at me with that radiant smile: "Gabriella, I'm here."

I stood very still against the doorframe to look at him. In spite of the warmth and light that filled the room I felt a touch of chill. *Where were you all those times when I needed you?* I thought. Yet he was just the same as ever: dark hair, brown, brown eyes, perfect teeth, that air of wealth so peculiar to men of his calling. If anything had changed, it was me. And then the reassurance of his smile, his casual confidence, the way he looked at me as though he could see straight through me—all my doubts—and these made me stronger in my resolve. I knew what answer I'd give when he asked me *that* question. Whatever else had happened in my life, I was his.

"When are you going to ask me?" I said. I hoped that my boldness wouldn't offend him, but I had to know.

He glanced from me to Goblin on top of the bookcase taking a catnap, to my crutches that leaned against the wall. "Tomorrow. Tomorrow at the riverside. I can send a car for you, Gabriella. I want you to be at the services. I want you to see exactly what I do before I ask you that question. Too many people have lied to you and hurt you in your life. I never want you to think I was one of them."

I loved him then more than I ever had before. If that was possible. "I'll be there."

"Worship starts at one, the healing at two. Could you come a little early . . . say at noon?"

"Eleven-thirty."

He gave me an elegant quizzical look, kissed the air above my face, and took his departure.

202

# 19

Everybody was there.

I hadn't been able to sleep at all the night before. As soon as the sun was up I rolled out of bed and went for a long dewy walk in the fields. Princess followed me, browsing on wildflowers and tender shoots, and Goblin ran ahead giving happy little cries as he jumped for butterflies or pounced on shadows in the jeweled grass. All I could think about that morning before the revival was *thank you, thank you, thank you.* I hoped that my brown-eyed young man would like cats. I hoped I could still be a teacher. I hoped that Oskar would still be my friend.

I arrived at the riverside in real style. Papa Joe would have been proud if he'd seen me. The car was long, black, and shiny as satin. It had me at my destination almost as soon as I'd climbed in, but even so it was close to noon when we arrived. I'd chosen one of the new dresses that Mama and I had made; it was white with a tiny print of bright red cherries, had a white stand-up collar of cotton piqué, and was designed to make me look tall and slim—which it couldn't do, of course, but it tried. I wanted Tim to like it. I wanted him to like *me*. I hoped and prayed that he wouldn't change his mind.

The Lockwoods were there, the Hagens, the Overbys, Olsons, Haagbloms, Nelsons, the Svensons, Hendrickssons, Andersons, and Halvorsons. The Halvorsons arrived in a jewel-toned Buick, ruby, with the price tag still glued in the window. They had to park far back on the road and walk to the revival tent, with its flags and banners lifting in the warm spring breeze. I hobbled along behind them on my crutches; I'd grown so weak and giddy with all the excitement I'd had to go back to them. I hoped Tim wouldn't mind, but then I thought of his exquisite kindness and I knew he would accept me, no matter what.

Beneath the huge circus tent canopy, strapping young farm boys were just setting up benches, row after row, and up front by the speaker's platform, a choir was forming, and a piano player rippled up and down the keys. I looked around for Mama and Papa Joe, but didn't see them. I had hoped that they would be there. I wanted them to see me, to see how I looked in my new white dress, to see how easily I could get along with and without my crutches. I wanted them to see how happy and successful I looked as I walked along with him. And of course I wanted them to share in my good news.

Oskar was there. He sat in one of the back rows, looking spruced up and spiffy in a starched shirt and dark green tie. He'd had a haircut, which only made his ears stick out the more. I'd told him, of course, why I was going to be here. I'd told him I was going to marry the preacher.

"You're sure you want to go through with this?" He looked pink and uncomfortable, as much from embarrassment as from the overhead sun. "This kind of life's not for you, Gabriella. You're much too good for all this."

"This is my life, Oskar. I've told you, I love him."

"You're making a big mistake."

"Wish me luck, anyway, won't you?"

"No," he said. "I won't."

His look of dismay stopped my heart. But then I looked up and saw Tim coming toward me, and my heart very nicely started up again.

"Gabriella? Where have you been? Who were you talking to? I've been frantic looking for you." He took me by the arm and hustled me toward the platform and behind a flap of canvas that formed a little tent inside the larger one. "I shouldn't be seen talking to you." He seemed strangely upset. "Gabriella, what I've got in mind is this: to show His healing power . . ." He glanced right and left, shot a look around the tent flap, came back again, and said, ". . . you've brought your crutches, good. Now, all you've got to do, Gabriella, is follow my instructions exactly . . . and believe that everything I tell you is true." He took my face in his two warm hands, and as the piano rippled up and down the keys, as the choir warbled and rose to hit the high notes, he looked deep into my eyes and said, "Believe . . . all I want you to do is believe . . . when I tell you to put down your crutches and walk, you will walk. You will walk straight and tall, and your steps will be even . . . you will not falter if you only believe."

And I did. I did believe. I knew that it could happen. I believed with all my heart and soul that I could do anything at all if he loved me. And he did love me . . . didn't he?

"Is that what you wanted to ask me?"

He drew back a little, that face I had dreamed of in my dreams, those strong hands; the brown eyes clouded just a little, but the music in the background went on the same.

"Is that what you wanted to ask me?" I knew what I was doing; I was asking the question that would destroy my fondest dream. "You wanted me to come forward to be healed, isn't that what you were going to ask me?"

"Why . . . yes, Gabriella. It was. I knew you wouldn't mind. It's for the Lord, for His glory . . . I thought you understood."

"I thought that you loved me . . ."

"But I do."

"But not in the way I love you." This was meant to be a question, but as I watched the understanding come into his lovely dark eyes, it became a statement. I'd been such a fool. And yet I had been healed, and because of him. I *was* loved, and I did love, and I knew that what he said was true: Belief had changed my life.

From our place offstage we could see the choir lining up, getting ready to take their places in the folding chairs behind the pulpit. Crowds of people had massed beneath the tent, ready to praise the Lord, ready to be healed by this same belief. They wanted to see me. They wanted to watch me stand up and walk without crutches, for if I could do it so could they give up whatever crutches they'd been dependent on.

"Think of it," Timothy was saying. "Think of all the good you could do."

"But I'm already cured, Tim. I'd be telling them a lie."

The music grew louder, fancier, more full of flourishes and grace notes adorning every bar. The choir stood and at full strength sang about the Lord and all His glory.

"How the people will love you," Timothy whispered, his breath as sweet as chamomile. "How they will cheer for you, and love you."

And I saw in my mind the little chariot and the costume Papa Joe had wanted for me, the little halo, the silken wings, and I said, "No."

"You won't?"

"No. I won't. I'm sorry, Tim, I really am, because it was you who made me strong, your faith, not mine."

Even in rage, his face was like the sun. I would love him always, always, but I could not do what he asked. Not then, not ever. I tucked my crutches under my arms and swung myself up from the metal chair, out of our private canvas place, down the long aisles, passing all the rows and rows of pleasant hopeful faces waiting to be loved as I had been. Waiting for an answer.

There is an answer. Sometimes.

Sometimes we're too deep in self-pity to hear it.

I'd like to say that Oskar met me outside the tent and offered me a ride back to the teacherage. I'd like to say he swung me up behind his saddle and carried me away, despite my desperate cries, but that was not the case. We were friends, then lovers, and we fought and broke up and we were friends again. But that is another story and has not yet come to its end.